I0651468

Richard Doddridge Blackmore

The Remarkable History of Sir Thomas Upmore, Bart., M.P.

Vol. 1

Richard Doddridge Blackmore

The Remarkable History of Sir Thomas Upmore, Bart., M.P.
Vol. 1

ISBN/EAN: 9783337222093

Printed in Europe, USA, Canada, Australia, Japan

Cover: Foto ©Raphael Reischuk / pixelio.de

More available books at **www.hansebooks.com**

THE REMARKABLE HISTORY

OF

SIR THOMAS UPMORE, BART., M.P.,

FORMERLY KNOWN AS

"TOMMY UPMORE."

Non usitatâ, non tenui ferar
Pennâ——

IN TWO VOLUMES.
VOL. I.

LONDON:

SAMPSON LOW, MARSTON, SEARLE & RIVINGTON,
CROWN BUILDINGS, 188, FLEET STREET.
1884.

PREFACE.

When Sir Thomas Upmore came, and asked me to write a short account of his strange adventures, I declined that honour; partly because I had never seen any of his memorable exploits. Perhaps that matters little, while his history so flourishes, because of being more creditable, as well as far more credible, than that of England, for the last few years.

Still, in such a case, the man who did the thing is the one to tell it. And his veracity has now become a proverb.

My refusal seemed to pain Sir Thomas, because he is so bashful; and no one can see him pained, without grieving for his own sake also, and trying to feel himself in the wrong.

This compelled me to find other arguments; which I did as follows :—

"First, my dear sir, in political matters, my

humble views are not strong, and trenchant—
as yours are become by experience—but exceedingly large, and lenient; because I have
never had anything at all to do with politics.

"Again, of science,—the popular name for
almost any speculation, bold enough,—I am in
ignorance equally blissful, if it were not thrilled
with fear. What power shall resist the wild
valour of the man, who proves that his mind
is a tadpole's spawn, and then claims for that
mind supreme dominion, and inborn omnisci-
ence? Before his acephalous rush, down go
piled wisdom of ages, and pinnacled faith, cloud-
capped heights of immortal hope, and even the
mansions everlasting, kept for those who live
for them."

"All those he may upset," replied Sir
Thomas, with that sweet and buoyant smile,
which has saved even his supernatural powers,
from the grudge of those less capable; "or at
least, he may fancy that he has done it. But
to come to facts,—can he upset, or even make
head, or tail, of such a little affair as I am?
Not one of his countless theories about me has

a grain of truth in it; though he sees me, and
feels me, and pokes me in the side, and listens,
as if I were a watch run down, to know whether
I am going.   I assure you, that to those who are
not frightened by his audacity, and fame, his
'links of irrefragable proof' are but a baby's
dandelion chain.   In chemistry alone, and engineering, has science made much true advance.
The main of the residue is arrogance."

"In that branch of science, we are all Professors," I answered, to disarm his wrath;
knowing that, in these riper years, honest indignation wrought upon his system, as youthful
exultation once had done; and I could not
afford to have a hole made in my ceiling.
"However, Sir Thomas, I shall stick to my
resolve.   Though your life—when its largeness
is seen aright—will be an honour to the history
of our race, justice comes before honour; and
only you can do justice to it."

Humility, which competes with truth, for the
foremost place in his character, compelled him
to shake his head at this; and he began again,
rather sadly.

"My purpose is a larger one, than merely to talk of my own doings. I want to put common sense into plain English, and to show—as our medical men show daily—that the body is beyond the comprehension of the mind. The mind commands the body to lie down, and be poked at, and probed, and pried into, with fifty subtle instruments, or even to be cut up, and analysed alive; and then what more has it ascertained? If the mind can learn nothing of the body it lives in, grows, rejoices, and suffers with, how can it know all about it, for millions of years, before either existed? How can it trace their joint lineage up to a thing, that had neither a head, nor a body?

"Go to: what I offer is not argument, but fact; and I care not the head of their ancestor for them. But if I write it, will you remove whatever may offend a candid mind?"

"If you offend that mind alone," said I. being fresh from a sharp review of something I had written; "you will give small offence indeed; and to edit you will be a sinecure."

R. D. BLACKMORE.

CONTENTS OF VOL. I.

TOMMY UPMORE.

———◦◦◦———

CHAPTER I.

SIGNS OF EMINENCE.

If I know anything of mankind, one of them needs but speak the truth to secure the attention of the rest, amazed as they are at his doing a thing far beyond their own power and experience. And I would not have troubled any one's attention, if I could only have been let alone, and not ferreted as a phenomenon.

When the facts, which I shall now relate, were fresh and vivid in the public mind. it might have been worth twenty guineas to me to set them in order and publish them. Such curiosity, then, was felt, and so much of the purest science talked, about my "abnormal organism," that nine, or indeed I may say ten, of the leading British publishers went so far as to offer me £20,* with a chance of five dollars from America, if I would only write my history!

But when a man is in full swing of his doings and his sufferings, how can he stop to set them down, for the pleasure of other people? And even now, when, if I only tried, I could do almost as much as ever, it is not with my own consent that you get this narrative out of me. How that comes to pass, you shall see hereafter.

Every one who knows me will believe that I have no desire to enlarge a fame, which already is too much for me. My desire is rather to slip away from the hooks and crooks of inquirers, by leaving them nothing to lay hold of, not even a fibre to retain a barb; myself remaining like an open jelly, clear, and fitter

* Sir Thomas cannot be accepted here, without a good-sized grain of salt. Exciting as his adventures are, and sanguine as his nature is, what can he be thinking of, in the present distress of publishers, strict economy of libraries, and bankruptcy of the United States?

for a spoon than fork,—as there is said to be a fish in Oriental waters, which, being hooked, turns inside out, and saves both sides by candour.

One reason why I now must tell the simple truth, and be done with it, is that big rogues have begun to pile a pack of lies about me, for the sake of money. They are swearing one another down, and themselves up, for nothing else than to turn a few pounds out of me ; while never a one of them knows as much as would lie on a sixpence about me. Such is the crop of crop-eared fame !

Now, if there is any man so eminent as to be made money of, surely he ought to be allowed to hold his own pocket open. Otherwise, how is he the wiser for all the wonder concerning him ? And yet those fellows, I do assure you, were anxious to elevate me so high, that every sixpence pitched at me should jump down into their own hats. This is not to my liking ; and I will do my utmost to prevent it. And when you know my peculiar case, you will say that I have cause for caution.

So fleeting is popularity, such a gossamer the clue of history, that within a few years of the time when I filled a very large portion of the public eye, and was kept in great type at every journal office, it may even be needful for me to remind a world, yet more volatile than myself, of the thrilling sensation I used to create, and the great amazement of mankind.

These were more natural than wise; for I never was a wonder to myself, and can only hope that a truthful account of my trouble will commend me, to all who have time enough to think, as a mortal selected by nature for an extremely cruel experiment, and a lesson to those who cannot enjoy her works, without poking sticks at them.

My father was the well-known Bucephalus Upmore—called by his best friends "Bubbly Upmore"—owner of those fine soap-boiling works, which used to be the glory of old Maiden Lane, St. Pancras. He was one of the best-hearted men that ever breathed, when things went according to his mind; blest with every social charm, genial wit, and the sur-

prising products of a brisk and poetical memory.
His figure was that of the broadest Briton, his
weight eighteen stone and a half, his politics
and manners Constitutional all over. At every
step he crushed a flint, or split a contractor's
paving-stone, and an asphalt walk was a
quagmire to him.

My mother also was of solid substance, and
very deep bodily thickness. She refused to be
weighed, when philosophers proposed it; not
only because of the bad luck that follows,
but also because she was neither a bull, nor
a pen of fat pigs, nor a ribboned turkey. But
her husband vouched her to be sixteen stone;
and if she had felt herself to be much less, why
should she have scorned to step into the scales,
when she understood all the rights of women?

These particulars I set down, simply as
a matter of self-defence, because men of
science, who have never seen me, take my case
to support their doctrine of "Hereditary
Meiocatobarysm," as they are pleased to call
it, presuming my father to have been a man
of small specific gravity, and my mother a

woman of levity. They are thoroughly welcome
to the fact, out of which they have made so
much, that the name of my mother's first
husband was Lightbody—Thomas Lightbody, of
Long Acre, a man who made springs for
coaches. But he had been in St. Pancras
churchyard, seven good years before I was born;
and he never was mentioned, except as a saint,
when my father did anything unsaintly.

But a truce to philosophy, none of which has
ever yet bettered my condition. Let every tub
stand, or if stand it cannot, let every tub fly
on its own bottom. Better it is to have no
attempt at explanation of my case, than a
hundred that stultify one another. And a truly
remarkable man has no desire to be explained
away.

Like many other people, who have contrived
to surprise the world before they stopped, I did
not begin too early. As a child, I did what
the other children did, and made no attempt
to be a man too soon. Having plenty of time
on my hands, I enjoyed it, and myself, without
much thought. My mother alone perceived that

nature intended me for greatness, because I
was the only child she had. And when I began
to be a boy, I took as kindly as any boy to
marbles, peg-top, tip-cat, toffy, lollipops, and
fireworks, the pelting of frogs, and even of dogs,
unless they retaliated, and all the other delights
included in the education of the London boy;
whose only remarkable exploit is to escape a
good hiding every day of his life.

But as a straw shows the way of the wind,
a trifle or two, in my very early years, gave
token of future eminence. In the days of my
youth, there was much more play than there
ever has been since; and we little youngsters
of Maiden Lane used to make fine running at
the game of "I spy," and even in set races.
At these, whenever there was no wind, I was
about on a par with the rest of my age, or
perhaps a little fleeter. But whenever a strong
wind blew, if only it happened to be behind my
jacket, Old Nick himself might run after me in
vain; I seemed not to know that I touched the
ground, and nothing but a wall could stop me.
Whereas, if the wind were in front of my

waistcoat, the flattest-footed girl, even Polly Windsor, could outstrip me.

Another thing that happened to me was this, and very unpleasant the effects were. My mother had a brother, who became my Uncle William, by coming home from sea, when everybody else believed him drowned and done for. Perhaps to prove himself alive, he made a tremendous noise in our house, and turned everything upside down, having a handful of money, and being in urgent need to spend it. There used to be a fine smell in our parlour, of lemons, and sugar, and a square black bottle; and Uncle William used to say, "Tommy, I am your Uncle Bill; come and drink my health, boy! Perhaps you will never see me any more." And he always said this in such a melancholy tone, as if there was no other world to go to, and none to leave behind him.

A man of finer nature never lived, according to all I have heard of him. Wherever he might be, he regarded all the place as if it were made for his special use, and precisely adapted for his comfort; and yet as if something was always coming, to make him say "good-bye" to it. He had an extraordinary faith in luck, and when it turned against him, off he went.

One day, while he was with us, I came in with an appetite ready for dinner, and a tint of outer air upon me, from a wholesome play on the cinder-heaps. "Lord, bless this Tommy," cried Uncle William; "he looks as if he ought to go to heaven!" And without another word, being very tall and strong, he caught hold of me under the axle of my arms, to give me a little toss upward. But instead of coming down again, up I went, far beyond the swing of his long arms. My head must have gone into the ceiling of the passage, among the plaster and the laths; and there I stuck fast by the peak of my cap, which was strapped beneath my chin with Spanish leather. To see, or to cry, was alike beyond my power, eyes and mouth being choked with dust; and the report of those who came running below is that I could only kick. However, before I was wholly done for, somebody fetched the cellar-steps, and with very great difficulty pulled me down.

Uncle William was astonished more than anybody else, for everybody else put the blame upon him; but he was quite certain that it never could have happened, without some fault on my part. And this made a soreness between him and my mother, which (in spite of his paying the doctor's bill for my repairs, as he called it) speedily launched him on the waves again, as soon as his money was got rid of.

This little incident confirmed my mother's already firm conviction that she had produced a remarkable child. "The Latin Pantheon is the place for Tommy," she said to my father, every breakfast time; "and to grudge the money, Bucephalus, is like flying in the face of Providence."

"With all my heart," father always answered, "if Providence will pay the ten guineas a quarter, and £2 15s. for extras."

"If you possessed any loftiness of mind," my mother used to say, while she made the toast, "you would never think twice of so low a thing as money, against the education of your only child; or at least you would get them to take it out in soap."

"How many times must I tell you, my dear, that every boy brings his own quarter of a pound? As for their monthly wash, John Windsor's boy, Jack, is there, and they get it out of him."

"That makes it so much the more disgraceful," my mother would answer, with tears in her eyes, "that Jack Windsor should be there, and no Tommy Upmore! We are all well aware that Mr. Windsor boils six vats for one of ours; and sixty, perhaps, if he likes to say it. But, on the other hand, he has six children against our one; and which is worth the most?"

My father used to get up nearly always, when it came to this, and take his last cup standing, as if his work could not wait for him. However, it was forced into his mind, more and more every morning, that my learning must come to a question of hard cash, which he never did approve of parting with. And the more he had to think of it, the less he smiled about it. At

last, after cold meat for dinner three days
running, he put his best coat on and walked off
straightway for the *Parthencion*, which is in Ball's
Pond, Islington. He did not come home in at
all a good temper, but boiled a good hour after
boiling time, and would not let any one know,
for several days, what had gone amiss with him.

For my·part, having, as behoves a boy, no
wild ambition to be educated, and hearing from
Jack Windsor what a sad case he was in, I
played in the roads, and upon the cinder-hills,
and danced defiance at the classic pile, which
could be seen afar sometimes, when the smoke
was blowing the other way. But while I was
playing, sad work went on, and everything was
settled without my concurrence. Mrs. Rumbelow herself, the Doctor's wife, lady president
of the college, although in a deeply interesting state—as dates will show hereafter—not
only came in a cab to visit my mother, but
brought with her on the dicky, as if he were
nobody, the seventh nephew of the Lord Mayor
of London, who could do a Greek tree, if it was
pencilled out.

This closed all discussion, and clenched my fate, and our tailor was ordered to come next morning. My father had striven his utmost to get me taken as a day-boy, or at any rate to be allowed to keep a book against the Muses. But Mrs. Rumbelow waved her hand, and enlarged upon liberal associations, and the higher walks of literature, to such an extent that my father could not put a business foot in anywhere. And before I was sent to bed that night, when I went for my head to be patted, and to get a chuck below the chin, he used words which hung long in my memory.

"Poor Tommy, thy troubles are at hand;" he said, with a tender gaze at me beneath his pipe. "They can't make no profit from the victualling of thy mind; but they mean to have it out of thy body, little chap. 'Tis a woe as goes always to the making of a man. And the Lord have mercy on thee, my son Tommy!"

CHAPTER II.

ITUR AD ASTRA.

The grandest result of education is the revival of the human system, which ensues when it is over. If it be of all pangs the keenest to remember joy in woe, and of all pleasures the sweetest to observe another's travail, upon either principle, accommodated (as all principles are) to suit the purpose, how vast the delight of manhood in reflecting upon its boyhood!

Dr. Rumbelow, of the *Partheneion,* which is in Trotter's Lane, Ball's Pond, combined high gifts of nature with rich ornaments of learning. In virtue of all this, he strove against the tendency of the age towards flippancy, and self-indulgence, the absence of every high principle, and the presence of every low one. Having to

fill both the heads and the stomachs of thirty-
five highly respectable boys, he bestirred himself
only in the mental part, and deputed to others
the bodily—not from any greed, or want of
feeling, but a high-minded hatred of business,
and a lofty confidence in woman. So well
grounded was this faith, that Mrs. Rumbelow
never failed to provide us with fine appetites.

Here, and hence, I first astonished the weak
minds of the public, and my own as much as
anybody's. Although we had several boys of
birth, the boy of largest brains and body took
the lead of all of us. And this was Bill Chumps,
now Sir William Chumps, the well-known M.P.
for St. Marylebone. His father was what was
then called a "butcher," but now a "purveyor of
animal provisions." He supplied under contract
the whole *Partheneion;* and his meat was so
good that we always wanted more.

Bill Chumps, being very quick at figures, had
made bright hits about holidays impending, by
noting the contents of the paternal cart, and
blowing the Sibylline leaves of the meat-book,
handed in by the foreman. But even Chumps

was not prepared for a thing that happened one fine Friday.

We had been at work all the afternoon, or, at any rate, we had been in school; and a longing for something more solid than learning began to rise in our young breasts.

"Oh, shouldn't I like a good pig's fry?" the boy next to me was whispering.

"Or a big help out of a rump-steak pie?" said the fellow beyond him, with his slate-sponge to his mouth.

But Chumps said, "Bosh! What's the good of pigs and pastry? Kidneys, and mushrooms, is my ticket, Tommy. Give us the benefit of your opinion."

Chumps was always very good to me, although I was under his lowest waistcoat-button. For my father was a very good customer of that eminent butcher his father; not only when he wanted a choice bit of meat, but also as taking at a contract-price all bones that could not be sent out at a shilling a pound, as well as all the refuse fat, which now makes the best fresh butter.

In reply to that important question, I looked
up at Chumps, with a mixture of hesitation and
gratitude. Being a sensitive boy, I found it so
hard to give an opinion without offence to elder
minds, yet so foolish to seem to have no opinion,
and to spoil all the honour of being consulted.
A sense of responsibility made me pause, and
ponder, concerning the best of all the many good
things there are to eat, and to lay "mechani-
cally," as novelists express it, both hands upon
a certain empty portion of my organization,
when Dr. Rumbelow arose !

We did not expect him to get up yet for
nearly three-quarters of an hour, unless any
boy wanted caning; and at first a cold tremor
ran through our inmost bones, because we
respected him so deeply. But a glance at his
countenance reassured us. The doctor stood
up, with his college-cap on, a fine smile lifting
his gabled eyebrows (as the evening sun lights
up gray thatch), his tall frame thrown back, and
his terrible right hand peacefully, under his
waistcoat, loosening the button of didactic cinc-
ture. He spread forth the other hand, with no

cane in it; and a yawn—such as we should have
had a smack for—came to keep company with
his smile.

" Boys ! " he shouted, sternly at first, from
the force of habit when we made a noise; "boys,
Lacedæmonians, Partheneionidæ, hearken to the
words which I, with friendly meaning, speak
among you. It has been ordained by the powers
above, holding Olympian mansions, that all
things come in circling turn to mortal men who
live on corn. Times there are for the diligent
study of the mighty minds of old, such as we,
who now see light of sun, and walk the many-
feeding earth, may never hope to equal. But
again there are seasons, when the *dies festi*
must be held, and the *feriæ Latinæ*, which a
former pupil of mine translated ' a holiday from
Latin.' Such a season now is with us. Once
more it has pleased the good Lucina to visit our
humble *tugurium ;* and we are strictly called
upon to observe the *meditrinalia*. Since which
things are so, it behoves me to proclaim to all
of you *feriæ tridui imperativæ*."

The doctor's speech had been so learned, that

few of us were able to make out his meaning.
But Chumps was a boy of vast understanding,
and extraordinary culture.

"Three days' holiday. Holloa, boys, holloa!"
cried Chumps, with his cap going up to the
roof. "Three days' holiday! Rump-steak for
breakfast, and lie a-bed up to nine o'clock.
Hurrah, boys! holloa louder, louder, louder!
Again, again, again! Why, you don't half
holloa!"

To the ear of reason it would have been
brought home, that the boys were holloaing quite
loud enough; and of that opinion was our
master, who laid his hands under his silvery
locks, while the smile of good-will to us, whom
he loved and chastened, came down substan-
tially to the margin of his shave. But behold,
to him thus beholding, a new and hitherto
unheard-of prodigy, wonderful to be told, arose!
He sought for his spectacles, and put them on;
and then for his cane, and laid hold of it —
because he beheld going up into the air, and
likely to get out of his reach, a boy!

It is not for me to say how I did it. Nobody

was more amazed than I was; although after all that had happened ere now to me, I might have been prepared for it. Much as I try to remember what my feelings were, all I can say is that I really know not; and perhaps the confusion produced by going round so (to which I was not yet accustomed), and of looking downward at the place I used to stand on, helped to make it hard for me to think what I was up to.

With no consideration, as to what I was about, and no sense of being out of ordinary ways, I found myself leaving all the ground, and its places, not with any jump, or other kind of rashness, but gently, equably, and in good balance, rising to the shoulders of the other little chaps, and then over the heads of the tallest ones. My sandals, because of the weather being warm, were tied with light-blue ribbon, according to the wishes of my mother; and these made a show which I looked down at, while everybody else stared up at them.

Chumps was a very tall boy for his age, by reason of all the marrow-bones he got; and the same thing had gifted him with high courage.

So that while all the other boys could only stare, or run away, if their nerves were quick, he made a spring with both hands at my feet, to fetch me back to the earth again. And at the same instant he said, "Tommy!" in the very kindest tone of voice, entreating me to come down to him.

I do not exaggerate in saying that I strove with all my power to do this; and with his kind help I might have done it, if the string of my shoe had been sewed in. But unhappily, like most things now, it was made for ornament more than use; and so it slipped out and was left in his hand; while, much against my will, I rose higher and higher. At the same time I found myself going round and round, so that I could not continue to observe the countenance of Dr. Rumbelow, gazing sternly, and with some surprise, at me. But I saw him put on his spectacles, which was always a bad sign for us.

"*Capnobatæ* is the true reading in Strabo, as I have so long contended. Fetch me a cane! —a long, long, cane!" the doctor shouted, as I still went up. "This is the spirit of the rising age! I have long expected something of this kind. I will quell it, if I have to tie three canes together. Thomas Upmore, come down, that I may cane you. Not upon my head, boy, or how can I do it?"

For no sooner had I heard what was likely to befall me, than my heart seemed to turn into a lump of cold lead. At once my airy revolutions ceased, my hands (which had been hovering like butterflies) stopped, and dropped, like beetles that have struck against a post, and down I came plump, with both feet upon the tassel of the trencher-cap upon the doctor's head.

This must have been a very trying moment, both for his patience and my courage, and it is not fair to expect me to remember everything that happened. However, I feel that if I had been caned, there would have been a mark upon my memory; even as boys bear the limits of the parish in their minds, through their physical geography. Likely enough my head was giddy, from so much revolving; and Chumps living near us marched me home, with a big lexicon strapped on my back, to prevent me from trying to fly again.

CHAPTER III.

Most people, and more especially our writers of fiction, history, philosophy, and so forth, indulge in reflection, at those moments, when they are soaring above our heads ; but I have always found myself so unlucky in this matter, as in many others, that nothing would ever come into my head, when aloft, to be any good when I came down. Or, at least only once, as will be shown hereafter ; and that was the exception, which proves the rule.

Otherwise, I might now give many nice and precise descriptions of " variant motions and emotions, both somatic and psychical "—as Professor Brachipod expressed them—which must, according to his demonstration, have been inside

me, at my first flight. Very likely they were:
and even if they were not, it would never pay
me to be positive—or negative perhaps is the
proper word now—because ignorant science is
remunerative, and nothing can be got by im-
pugning it.

Yet that consideration, I assure you, has
nothing to do with my present silence. I am
silent, simply because I know nothing; and if
all so placed would try my plan, how much less
would be said and written! Nevertheless all
biologists, psychologists, anthropologists, and
the rest of our race who make it their study
(after proving it wholly below their heed) these
men, if they deign to be called such, have a
claim upon me for all my facts; which I will not
grudge, when I know them.

From the very outset, they felt this; and my
father and mother, who had not slept well,
through talking so much of my above adventure
—recounted perhaps with some embellishment
by Chumps—hardly had got through their
breakfast before some eminent " scientists " were
at them. For my part, having made a hearty

supper, (after long scarcity of butcher's meat,) or perhaps from having swallowed so much air, I had slept long and soundly, and was turning for another good sleep, when I heard great voices.

" Madam, allow me to express surprise," were the words which came up to me, through the ceiling, at the place where my head had made the hole, " extreme surprise at the narrowness of your views. Must I come to the conclusion, that you refuse to forward the interests of science ? "

" Sir," replied mother, who was always polite, when she failed to make out what people meant, " science is what I don't know from the moon. But I do know what my Tommy is."

" My dear Mrs. Upmore," was the answer, in a soft sweet voice, which I found afterwards to be that of Professor Brachipod, " in consulting the interests of science, we shall consult those of the beloved Tommy. His existence is so interwoven with a newly formed theory of science "——

" You impudent hop'-my-thumb, what do you mean," broke in a deep sound, which I knew to be my father's, " by calling my wife your dear indeed? First time as ever you set eyes on her. Out you go, and no mistake."

Upon this ensued a heavy tread, and a little unscientific squeak; and out went Professor Brachipod, as lightly as if on the wings of his theory.

"Upmore, this violence is a mistake," another and larger voice broke in, as my father came back quietly; "the Professor's views may be erroneous; but to eliminate him, because of somatic inferiority, is counter to the tendency of the age. My theory differs from his, *toto cœlo*. But in the cause of pure reason, I protest against unmanly recourse to physics."

"You shall have the same physick, if you don't clear out;" said my father, as peaceable a man as need be, till his temper was put up; "an Englishman's house is his castle. No science have a right to come spoiling his breakfast. You call me unmanly, in your big words. You are a big man, and now I'll tackle you. Out goes Professor Jargoon."

There was some little scuffle, before this larger Professor was "eliminated," because he was a strong man, and did not like to go ; but without much labour he was placed outside.

"Now, if either of you two chaps comes back," my father shouted from his threshold, "the science he gets will be my fist. And lucky for him, he haven't had it yet."

Running to the window of my room, I saw the professors, arm-in-arm, going sadly up the cinder-heaps; and glad as I was to be quit of them, I did not like the way of it. However, I hoped for the best, and went down in my trousers and braces to breakfast. My father was gone to his boiling by this time, for nothing must ever interfere with that; but my mother would never give up her breakfast, till she saw the bottom of the teapot.

"Oh, Tommy darling," she cried, as she caught me, and kissed me quite into the china-cupboard, for we always had breakfast in the kitchen, when out of a maid-of-all-work : "my own little Tommy, do you know why you fly ? All the greatest men in the kingdom have been here, to prove that you do it from reasons of Herod, Heroditical something—but he was a

bad man, and murdered a million of little ones.
They may prove what they like; and of course
they know more about my own child, than 1 do.
I don't care that for their science," said mother,
snapping her thumb, which was large and very
fat; "but tell me, Tommy, from your own dear
feelings, what it was that made you fly so?"

"I didn't fly, mother; I only went up, because
I could not help it. Because I was so empty,
and felt certain of getting full again, quite
early in the holidays."

"Begin at once, darling, and don't talk. Oh,
it is a cruel, cruel thing, that you should leave
the ground for want of victuals, when your father
clears eight pounds a week. Deny it as he may,
I can prove it to him. But I have found out
what makes you fly. A flip for their science, and
thundering words!"

"Well, mother, I don't want to do it again;"
I answered as well as I could, with my mouth
quite full of good bacon, and a baker's roll;
"but do please tell me what made me do it."

"Tommy, the reason is out of the Bible.
You cannot help flying, just because you are an
angel."

"They never told me that at school," I said; "and old Rum would have caned me, if he could reach. But he never would have dared to cane an angel."

"Hush, Tommy, hush! How dare you call that learned old gentleman, with white hair, 'old Rum'? But never mind, darling. Whatever you do, don't leave off eating."

For this I might be trusted, after all I had been through; and so well did I spend my days at home (especially when Bill Chumps came to dine with us, upon his own stipulation what the dinner was to be), that instead of going up into the air at all, the stoutest lover of his native land could not have surpassed me in sticking to it.

Chumps, though the foremost of boys, was inclined to be shy with grown-up people, till mother emboldened him with ginger-wine, and then he gave such an account of my exploit, that my father, and mother, looked at him with faces as different as could be. My mother's face was all eyes and mouth, with admiration, delight, excitement, vigorous faith, and desire for more; my father's face was all eyebrows, nose, and lips; and he shook his big head, that neighbour Chumps should have such a liar for his eldest son. Nothing but the evidence of his own eyes would ever convince Bucephalus Upmore, that a son of his, or of any other Englishman, came out of an egg; without which there was no flying.

"Mr. Upmore, you should be ashamed of yourself," my mother broke in rather sharply, " to argue such questions before young boys. But since you must edify us, out with your proof that the blessed angels were so born. Or will you deny them the power to fly?"

" Never did I claim," answered father, with a little wink at Chumps, " to know the ins and outs of angels, not having married one, as some folk do, until they discover the difference. Our Tommy is a good boy enough, in his way; but no angel, no more than his parents be. If ever I see him go up like a bubble, I'll fetch him down sharp with my clout-rake; but if I don't use my rake till then, it will last out my life-time, I'll bet a guinea. Now, Tommy, feed, and don't talk or look about. You'll be sorry when you get back to school, for every moment that you have wasted."

"My mind is not altogether clear," said mother, "about letting him go back to the Latin Pantheon"—this was her name for the *Parthenæion* ; "he is welcome to have a gentle fly now and then, as Providence has so endowed him, and I am sure he would never fly away from his own mother ; but as for his flying, because he is empty in his poor inside—I'll not hear of it. Bucephalus, how would you like it ?"

"Can't say at all, mother, till I have tried it. Shall be glad to hear Tommy's next experience. Back he goes to-morrow morning ; and by this day week, if they starve him well, he'll be fit to go sky-high again. A likely thing, indeed, that I should pay ten guineas beforehand, for a quarter's board, and tuition in classics and mathematics, all of the finest quality, and another ten guineas in lieu of notice, and get only three weeks for the whole of it ! Come, Tommy, how much have you learned, my boy ?"

"Oh, ever such a lot, father ! I am sure I don't know what."

" Well, my son, give us a sample of it. Unless there's too much to break bulk at random. Tip us a bit of your learning, Tommy."

" Wait a bit, father, till I've got my fingers up. When they come right, I say *hic, hæc, hoc,* and the singular number of *musa,* a song. I have told mother every word of it."

"Out and out beautiful it sounds," said mother; " quite above business, and what goes on in the week. Dr. Rumbelow must be a wonderful man, to have made such great inventions."

" Well, it's very hard to pay for it, and leave it in the clouds," my father said, sniffling as if he smelled pudding. " Let's have some more of it, sky-high Tommy."

My mother looked at me, as much as to say, " Now, my dear son, astonish him"; and my conscience told me that I ought to do it; and I felt myself trying very hard indeed to think: but not a Latin word would come of it. Perhaps I might have done it, if it had not been for Chumps, who kept on putting up his mouth, to blow me some word, bigger than the one that I was after ; while all that I wanted was a little one. And father leaned back, with a wink, to encourage me to take the shine out of himself, by my learning. But I could only lick my spoon.

"Come, if that is ten guineas' worth of Latin," said my father, "I should like to know what sixpenn'orth is. Tell us the Latin for sixpence, Tommy."

It was natural that I should not know this ; and I doubt whether even Chumps did, for he turned away, lest I should ask him. But my mother never would have me trampled on.

"Mr. Upmore, you need not be vulgar," she said, "because you have had no advantages. Would you dare to speak so, before Latin scholars ? Even Master Chumps is blushing for you ; and his father a man of such fine common sense ! No sensible person can doubt, for a moment, that Tommy knows a great many words of Latin, but is not to be persecuted out of them, in that very coarse manner, at dinner-time. Tell me, my dear," she said, turning to me, for I was fit to cry almost, "what is the reason that you can't bring out your learning. I am sure that you have it, my chick; and there must be some very good reason for keeping it in."

" Then, I'll tell you what it is," I answered, looking at my father, more than her; " there is such a lot of it, it all sticks together."

" That's the best thing I ever heard in my life;" cried father, as soon as he could stop laughing, while Chumps was grinning wisely, with his mouth full of pudding. " What a glorious investment of my ten guineas, to have a son so learned, that he can't produce a word of it, because it all sticks together! To-morrow, my boy, you shall go back for the rest of it. Like a lump of grains it seems to be, that you can't get into with a mashing-stick. Ah, I shall tell that joke to-night!"

" So you may," said mother, " so you may, Bucephalus; but don't let us have any more of it. 'Tis enough to make any boy hate learning, to be blamed for it, so unjustly. Would he ever have flown, if it had not been for Latin? And that shows how much he has got of it. Answer that, if you can, Mr. Upmore."

But my father was much too wise to try. "Sophy, you beat me there," he said; "I never was much of a hand at logic, as all the clever ladies are. Bill Chumps shall have a glass of wine after his pudding, and Tommy drink water like a flying fish; and you may pour me a drop from the black square bottle, as soon as you have filled my pipe, my dear."

"That I will, Bucephalus, with great pleasure; if you will promise me one little thing. If Tommy goes back to that Latin Pantheon, they must let him come home, every Sunday."

"Fly home to his nest, to prevent him from flying;" my father replied, with a smile of good humour, for he liked to see his pipe filled; "encourage his crop, and discourage his wings. 'Old Rum,' as they call him, wouldn't hear of that at first. But perhaps he will, now that he has turned out such a flyer."

CHAPTER IV.

THE PURSUIT OF SCIENCE.

MANY people seem to find the world grow
worse, the more they have of it ; that they may
be ready to go perhaps to a higher and better
region.   But never has this been the case with
me, although I am a staunch Conservative.   My
settled opinion is that nature (bearing in her
reticule the human atom) changes very slowly,
so that boys are boys, through rolling ages ;
even as Adam must have been, if he had ever
been a boy.

At any rate, the boys at Dr. Rumbelow's were
not so much better than boys are now, as to
be quoted against them.   They certainly seem
to have had more courage, more common-sense,
and simplicity, together with less affectation,

daintiness, vanity, and pretension. But, on the other hand, they were coarser, wilder, and more tyrannical, and rejoiced more freely than their sons do now, in bullying the little ones. The first thing a new boy had to settle was his exact position in the school; not in point of scholarship, or powers of the mind, but as to his accomplishments at fisticuff. His first duty was to arrange his school-fellows in three definite classes—those who could whack him and he must abide it, those he would hit again if they hit him, and those he could whack without any danger, whenever a big fellow had whacked him. Knowledge of the world, and of nature also, was needed for making this arrangement well : to over-esteem, or to undervalue self, brought black eyes perpetual, or universal scorn.

But to me, alas, no political study of this kind was presented. All the other boys could whack me, and expostulation led to more. Because I was the smallest, and most peaceful, among all the little ones, and the buoyancy of my nature made a heavy blow impossible. Yet upon the whole, the others were exceedingly kind and good

157072

to me, rejoicing to ply me with countless nick-
names, of widely various grades of wit, suggested
by my personal appearance, and the infirmity of
lightness. Tom-tit, Butterfly-Upmore, Flying
Tommy, and Skylark, were some of the names
that I liked best, and answered to most freely ;
while I could not bear to be called Soap-suds,
Bubbly, Blue-bottle, or Blow-me-tight. But
whatever it was, it served its turn ; and the
boy, who had been witty at my expense, felt less
disposed to knock me.

But, even as with the full-grown public,
opinion once formed is loth to budge, so with
these boys it was useless to argue, that having
flown once, I could not again do it. If they
would have allowed me simply to maintain the
opposite, or to listen mutely to their proofs, it
would have been all right for either side. But
when they came pricking me up, with a pin in
the end of a stick, or a two-pronged fork (such
as used to satisfy a biped with his dinner, and
a much better dinner then he gets now), endeavouring also to urge me on high, by an elevating
grasp of my hair and ears, you may well believe

me, when I say how sadly I lamented my exploit
above. I was ready to go up, I was eager to go
up; not only to satisfy public demand, but also
to get out of the way of it; and more than once
I did go up, some few inches, in virtue of the
tugs above, and pricks in lower parts of me.
But no sooner did I begin to rise, with general
expectation raised, and more forks ready to go
into me, than down I always came again, calling
in vain for my father and mother, because I
could not help it.

Upon such occasions, no one had the fairness
to allow for my circumstances. Every one
vowed that I could fly as well as ever, if I tried
in earnest; and I was too young to argue with
them, and point out the real cause; to wit
the large and substantial feeding, in which I
employed my Sundays. By reason of this I
returned to school, every Monday morning, with
a body as heavy as my mind almost; and to
stir up either of them was useless, for a long time
afterwards.

As ill luck would have it, it was on a Monday,
that science made her next attack on me. And

now let me say, that if ever you find me (from your own point of view) uncandid, bigoted, narrow-minded, unsynthetical, unphilosophical, or anything else that is wicked and low, when it fails to square with theories,—in the spirit of fair play you must remember what a torment science has been to me.

Five of them came, on that Monday afternoon, four in a four-wheeler, and one on the dicky: and we had a boy who could see things crooked, through some peculiar cast of eye, and though the windows were six feet over his head, he told us all about it, and we knew that he was right.

Presently in came the doctor's page (a boy who was dressed like Mercury, but never allowed in the schoolroom, unless he had urgent cause to show); his name was Bob Jackson, and we had rare larks with his clothes, whenever we got hold of him—and he waved above his head, as his orders were to do, a very big letter for the doctor. Every boy of us rushed into a certainty of joy—away with books, and away to play! But woe, instead of bliss, was the order of the day. Dr. Rumbelow never allowed himself to be hurried, or flurried, by anything, except the appearance of his babies; and when he was made, as he was by and by, a Bishop, for finding out something in Lycophron, that nobody else could make head or tail of, he is said to have taken his usual leisure, in loosing the button enforced by Mrs. Rumbelow, ere ever he broke the Prime Minister's seal.

"Boys," he said now, after looking at us well, to see if anybody wanted caning, "lads who combine the discipline of Sparta with the versatile grace of Athens, Mr. Smallbones will now attend to you. Under his diligent care, you will continue your studies eagerly. In these degenerate days, hard science tramples on the arts more elegant. Happy are ye, who can yet devote your hours to the lighter muses. At the stern call of science (who has no muse, but herself is an Erinnys), I leave you in the charge of Mr. Smallbones. Icarillus, you will follow me, and bring the light cane, with the ticket No. 7. A light cane is sweeter for very little boys."

My heart went down to my heels, while bearing

my fate in my hands, I followed him. Conscience
had often reproached me, for not being able to
fly, to please the boys. Universal consent had
declared that it all was my fault, and I ought to
pay out for it. What was the use of my trying
to think that the world was all wrong, and myself
alone right? Very great men, like Athanasius,
might be able to believe it; but a poor little
Tommy like me could not. But I tried hard to
say to the doctor's coat-tails, "Oh, please not
to do it, sir, if you can please to help it."

Dr. Rumbelow turned, as we crossed a stone
passage (where my knees knocked together from
the want of echo, and a cold shiver crept into my
bones), and, seeing the state of my mind and
body, and no boy anywhere near us, he could
not help saying, "My poor Icarillus, cheer up,
rouse up, *tharsei!* The Romans had no brief
forms of encouragement, because they never
required it. But the small and feeble progeny
of this decadent country— Don't cry, brave
Icarillus; don't cry, poor little fellow; none
shall touch you but myself. What terror hath
invaded you?"

The doctor stooped, and patted my head, which was covered with thick golden curls, and I raised my streaming eyes to him, and pointed with one hand at the cane, which was trembling in my other hand. My master indulged in some Latin quotation, or it may have been Greek for aught I know, and then translated, and amplified it, as his manner was with a junior pupil.

"Boys must weep. This has been ordained most wisely by the immortal gods, to teach them betimes the lesson needed in the human life, more often than any other erudition. But, alas for thee, poor Icaridion! it seems, as from the eyes afar, a thing unjust, and full of *thambos*. For thou hast not aimed at, nor even desired, the things that are unlawful, but rather hast been ensnared therein, by means of some necessity hard to be avoided. Therefore I say again, cheer up, Tommy! Science may vaunt herself, as being the mistress of the now happening day, and of that which has been ordained to follow; but I am the master of my own cane. Thomas Upmore, none shall smite thee."

A glow of joy came into my heart, and dried

up my tears in a wink or two, for we knew him to be a true man of his word, whether to cane, or to abstain; and if the professors had kept in the background, I might have soared up for them, then and there. But it never is their nature to do that; and before I had time to be really happy, four out of the five were upon me. Hearing the doctor's fine loud voice, they could no more contain themselves, but dashed out upon us, like so many dragons, on the back of their own eminence—Professors Brachipod, and Jargoon, Chocolous, and Mullicles; than whom are none more eminent on the roll of modern science. The fifth, and greatest of them all, whose name shall never be out-rubbed by time, but cut deeper every year, Professor Megalow, sat calmly on a three-legged stool, which he had found.

None of these learned gentlemen had seen my little self before; and an earnest desire arose in my mind, that not one of them ever should see me again. Their eyes were beaming with intellect, and their arms spread out like sign-posts; and I made off at once, without waiting to think, till the doctor's deep voice stopped me.

"Icarillus," he said, and though he could not catch them, my legs could go no further, "Athena, the Muses, and Phœbus himself, command thee to face the enemy. This new, and prosaic, and uncouth power, which calls itself 'science,' as opposed to learning, wisdom, and large philosophy—excuse me, gentlemen, I am speaking in the abstract—this arrogant upstart is so rampant, because people run away from her. Tommy, come hither; these gentlemen are kind, very kind—don't be afraid, Tommy; you may stand in the folds of my gown, if you like. Answer any question they may ask, and fly again, if they can persuade you. Professors Brachipod, and Jargoon, Chocolous, and Mullicles, my little pupil is at your service."

Beginning to feel my own importance, I began to grow quite brave almost, and ventured to take down my hands from my face, and turn round a little, and peep from the corners of my eyes at these great magicians. And as soon as I saw, that the foremost of them had been carried

out of our house by father, and sent away over
the cinder-heaps, there came a sort of rising in
my mind, which told me to try to stick up to
them. And when they fell out one with another,
as they lost no time in doing, they made me
think somehow about the old women who came
to pick over our ash-heaps—until through the
doorway I saw another face, the kindest and
grandest I ever had seen, the face of Professor
Megalow.

Before I had time to get afraid again, there
was no chance left to run away; for the four
professors had occupied all the four sides of my
body. They poked me, and pulled me in every
direction, and felt every tender part of me, and
would have been glad to unbutton my raiment,
if the master had allowed it. And they used
such mighty words as nobody may reproduce
correctly, unless he was born, or otherwise
endowed, with a ten-chain tape at the back of
his tongue. Every one talked, as fast as if the
rest were listening eagerly; and every one
listened, as much as if the rest had nought to
say to him. For all worked different walks of

science, and each was certain that the other's walk was crooked.

I assure you, that this was a very difficult thing for me to deal with, having so many tongues going on about me, and so many hands going into me, and a strong pull in one direction, crossed by a stronger push in the other. Moreover, two learned gentlemen wanted to throw me up perpendicular; while other two, of equal learning, would launch me on high horizontally. Between, and among, and amid them all, there was like to be nothing but specimens left of unfortunate Tommy Upmore.

"Gentlemen, gentlemen!" shouted Dr. Rumbelow; but they did not answer to that name. "Professors, professors, forbear, I beseech you. Is this scientific investigation? I will have no vivisection here"—for they hurt me so much, that I now screamed out—"I am sorry to lay hands upon you, but humanity compels me. Now, unless you all sit down, I shall send Argeiphontes for the police. I grieve that you drive me to such strong measures. But I cannot have my little Icarus treated like Orpheus, or Actæon."

Luckily for me the doctor's body might vie with his mind in grasp of subject; and he soon had Professors Brachipod, Jargoon, and Mullicles seated in their chairs. But the fourth professor (whose name was Chocolous, and himself a foreigner of some kind) entreated that he might not be compelled to sit.

"Not for five, six, seven year, have I seet in ze shair," he cried, with his arms spread out, and his back in a shake against some degradation; "I must not, and I will not, seet. Herr Doctor, in many languages laboriously excellent, present not to me zis grade indignity. I vill keek, if you not leave off."

He was very angry, but his friends seemed to enjoy it.

"Oblige me, gentlemen," said Dr. Rumbelow, decorously quitting this excitement, "by telling me, why your learned friend resists my kindly efforts. When the body is seated, the mind is calm. What find we in Plato upon that subject? Not only once, but even thrice, in a single dialogue, we discover, directly and inferentially——"

"A flip for those old codgers, sir!" exclaimed

Professor Brachipod. "Chocolous knows more than fifty Platos, though his leading idea is fundamentally erroneous "—("I say nah, I say non, I say bosh!" broke in Professor Chocolous)—"his leading idea that the human race may recover its primordial tail, by abstaining, for only a few generations——"

"Seven chenerations, first; and when he have attained one yoint, seven more. I am ze first. But in two, tree, four hundred year, continued in ze female line, wizout ever going upon ze shair——"

"Shut up, Chocolous!" broke in Professor Mullicles. "How can molecular accretion ever be affected by human habitude? 'Tis a simple inversion of the fundamental process. Every schoolboy now is perfectly aware, that the protoplasmatic anthropomorphism was a single joint of tail. Molecular accretion immediately commenced; and the result—is such a fellow as you are."

"And such a fellow as Professor Megalow," the little German answered, with quiet self-respect; "if I vos one, he vos ze oder. Professor Megalow, vot for, you stay back so?"

" My reason for staying back so, as our learned friend expresses it," said the tall man, with the kind and noble face, at last advancing, " is that the matter now in hand, though deeply interesting, and (to judge by results) even highly exciting, is one that I have never dealt with. When I was kindly asked to come, I was very glad to do so. But with your good leave, I will form no opinion; until I find some grounds for it."

The four men of science were struck dumb, at the rashness of such a resolution; while Dr. Rumbelow took advantage of their amazement, to say a word.

" Professor Megalow, allow me the honour of shaking hands with you, sir. You speak like a genuine acolyte of that glorious sage, Pythagoras. The ereneuticon, in all truth, must precede the hermeneuticon. Whenever you like to examine Tommy, he shall be at your service."

This offer was highly disinterested; but I did not enjoy its magnanimity, especially as my protector now became so engrossed with the great professor, that he quite forgot poor little me.

"Now is your time, to go through with the question," spake the arch-enemy, Brachipod, " which, beyond all doubt, is nothing more than a case of organic levigation——"

"Levigation be d—d!" cried Professor Jargoon. "Any fool can see, that it is gaseous expansion."

"Gaseous expansion is bosh, bosh, bosh," shouted Professor Chocolous ; " ze babe, zat vos born a veek longer dis day, vill tell you—bacilli, bacilli!"

"How pleasant it would be, to hear all this nonsense," declared Professor Mullicles, " if ignorance were not so dogmatic ! The merest neophyte would recognise, at once, this instance of histic fluxion."

Without any delay, a great uproar arose, and the four professors rushed at me, to save rushing at one another. My heart fell so low, that I could not run away, though extremely desirous of doing so; and the utmost I could manage was to get behind a chair, and sing out for my father and mother. This only redoubled their zeal, and I might not have been alive now to speak

of it, had not Professor Brachipod pulled out an
implement like a butcher's steelyard, and swung
back the others, with a sweep of it.

"He belongs to me. It was I who found him
out. I will have the very first turn at him," he
cried. "I'll knock on the head any man, who
presumes to prevent me from proving my theory.
Just hold him tight, while I get this steel hook
firmly into his collar. Now are you satisfied?
This proves everything. Can this levigation be
d—d, Jargoon? All his weight is a pound and
five ounces!"

He turned round in triumph, and a loud laugh
met him. He was weighing my jacket, without
me inside it. For mother had told me, a
hundred times, that a child had much better
be killed, than weighed. At the fright of his
touch, I slipped out of my sleeves, and set off
at the top of my speed away. In the passage,
I found a side door open, and without looking
back dashed through it.

"Go it, little 'un!" a cabman cried, the very
man who had brought mine enemies; and go it
I did, like a bird on the wing, without any know-

ledge of the ground below. Some of our boys, looking out of a window, called out, "Well done, Tommy! You'll win the—" something, it may have been the Derby, I went too fast to hear what it was. Short as my legs were, they flew like the spokes of a wheel that can never be counted; and I left a mail-cart, and a butcher's cart too, out of sight, though they tried to keep up with me. Such was my speed, on the wings of the wind, with my linen inflated, and my hair blown out,—the nimblest professor, that ever yet rushed to a headlong conclusion, were slow to me. In a word, I should have distanced all those enemies, had I only taken the right road home.

But alas, when I came to the top of a rise, from which I expected to see my dear parents, or at any rate our cinder-heap, there was nothing of the kind in sight. The breeze had swept me up the Barnet road; and yonder was the smoke of our chimney, like a streak, a mile away down to the left of me. All the foot of the hill, which is now panelled out into walls, and streets, of the great cattle-market, remained

to be crossed, without help of the wind, ere ever
I was safe inside our door. And the worst of
it was, that the ground had no cover,—not a
house, nor a tree, nor so much as a ditch, for
a smallish boy to creep along; only piles of
rubbish, here and there, and a few swampy
places, where snipes sometimes pitched down,
to have a taste of London.

Tired as I was, after that great run, and
scant of breath, and faint-hearted—for the
sun was gone down below Highgate Hill, and
my spirits ever seem to sink with him—I
started anew for my own sweet home, by the
mark of the smoke of our boiling-house. I
could hear my heart going pit-a-pat, faster
than my weary feet went; for the place was
as lonely as science could desire, for a snug
job of vivisection. Of that grisly horror I
knew not as yet the name, nor the meaning
precisely; but a boy at our school, who was
a surgeon's son, used to tell things, in bed,
there was no sleeping after. And once he had
said, "If they could catch you, Tommy, what
a treat you would be, to be lectured on!"

As the dusk grew deeper in the hollow places, and the ribs of the naked hills paler, I began to get more and more afraid, and to start back, and listen at my own footstep. And before I could hear what I hoped to hear—the anvil of the blacksmith down our lane—the air began to thicken with the recking of the earth, and the outline of everything in sight was blurred, and a very tired fellow could not tell, at any moment, what to run away from, without running into worse. At one time, I thought of sitting down, and hiding in a dip of the ground, till night came on, and my enemies could not see me; but although that might have been the safest plan, my courage would not hold out for it. So on I went, in fear and trembling, peeping, and peering, both behind me and before, and longing with all my heart to see our own door.

But instead of that, oh, what a sight I saw— the most fearful that can be imagined! From the womb of the earth, those four professors (whose names are known all over it), Brachipod, Jargoon, Chocolous, and Mullicles, came forth, and joined hands in front of me. They laughed, with a low scientific laugh, like a surgical blade on the grindstone.

"Capital, capital!" Brachipod cried; "we have got him all snug to ourselves, at last. Let me get my hook into my pretty little eel."

"Famous, famous!" said the deep voice of Jargoon; "now you shall see, how I work my compressor."

"Hoch, hoch!" chuckled Chocolous; "ve have catch ze leetle baird at last. I vill demonstrate his bacilli."

But the one that terrified me most of all was Professor Mullicles; because he said nothing, but kept one hand, upon something, that shone from his long black cloak.

"Oh, gentlemen, kind gentle gentlemen," I sobbed, dropping down on my knees before them, "do please let me go to my father, and mother. They live close by, and they think so much of me, and I am sure they would pay you, for all your inventions, a great deal more than the Government. I only flew once, and I didn't mean to fly, and I am sure it must have been a mistake altogether; and I will promise, upon my Sammy, as Bill Chumps says, not to do it any more. Oh, please to let me go! It is so late; and I beg your pardon humbly."

"Eloquent, and aerial Tommy," replied that dreadful Brachipod, "this case is too momentous, in the interests of pure science, for selfish motives to be recognized. It will be your lofty privilege, to abstract yourself, to revert to the age of unbroken continuity, when that which is now called Tommy was an atom of proto-bioplasm——"

"Stow that rubbish," broke in Jargoon.

"Ach, ach, ach! All my yaw is on the edge!" screamed Chocolous, dancing with his hands up.

"Proto-potatoes!" spoke Mullicles sternly, advancing to support his view of me.

"D—n," exclaimed all of them, unanimous for once, when there was no view of me to be had; "was there ever such a little devil? After him, after him! He can't get away."

"Can't he?" thought I, though I did not dare to speak, having not a single pant of breath to spare. For, while I was down on my knees for mercy, through the tears in my eyes, I had seen a lamp lit. I knew where that lamp was, and all about it, having broken the glass of it, once or twice, and lamps were a rarity in Maiden Lane as yet. It was not a quarter of a mile away, and the light of it shone upon my own white pillow.

So when those philosophers parted hands, to shake fists at one another, out of the scientific ring I slipped, and made off, for the life of me. My foes were not very swift of foot, and none of them would let another get before him; so that, if I had been fresh and bold, even without any breeze to help me, I might have outstripped them easily. But my legs were tired, and my mind dismayed; and the scientific terms, in which they called on me to stop, were enough to make any one stick fast. And the worst of it was, that having no coat on, I was very conspicuous in the dusk, and had no chance of dodging to the right or left. So that I could hear them gaining on me, and my lungs were too exhausted for me to scream out for father.

Thus, within an apple-toss of our back door, and with nothing but a down-hill slope, between

me and our garden, those four ogres of grim
science had me lapsing back into their grasp
again. Their hands were stretched forth, in
pursuit of my neck, and their breath was like
flame at the tips of my ears—when a merciful
Providence delivered me. I felt something
quivering under my feet; over which I went
lightly, with a puff of wind lifting the hollows
of my hair, and shirt-sleeves. In an instant, I
landed on a bank of slag; but behind me was a
fearful four-fold splash!

So absorbing was my terror, and so scattered
were my wits, that for ever so long I could not
make out, what had happened betwixt me and
my pursuers, except that I was safe, and they
were not. There they were, struggling, and
sputtering, and kicking—so much at least as
could be seen of them—throwing up their
elbows, or their heels, or heads, and execrating
nature (when their mouths were clear to do it)
in the very shortest language, that has ever
been evolved. At the same time, a smell (even
stronger than their words) arose, and grew so
thick, that they could scarcely be seen through it.

This told me, at once, what had befallen them, or rather what they had fallen into,—videlicet, the cleaning of our vats, together with Mr. John Windsor's; whose refuse and scouring is run away in trucks, upon the last Saturday of every other month. It would be hard to say, what variety of stench, and of glutinous garbage, is not richly present here; and the men from the sewers, who conduct it to the pit, require brandy, at short intervals. In the pit, which is not more than five feet deep, yet ought to be shunned by trespassers, the surface is covered with chloride of lime, and other materials, employed to kill smell, by outsmelling it; and so a short crust forms over it, until the contents become firm and slab, and can be cut out, for the good of the land, when the weather is cold, and the wind blows away.

Now certain it is, that all the science they were made of, could never have extricated those professors, without the strong arms of my father, and mother, and even small me at the end of the rope. The stuff they were in, being only half cooled (and their bodies grown sticky with

running so), fastened heavily on them, like
tallow on a wick, closing so completely both
mouth and eyes, that instead of giving, they
could only receive, a lesson in materialism.
Professors Brachipod, and Chocolous, being
scarcely five feet and a quarter in height, were
in great danger of perishing; but Mullicles, and
Jargoon, most kindly gave them a jump now and
then, for breath. And, to be quit of an unfra-
grant matter, and tell it more rapidly than we
did it,—with the aid of a blue-man from the
Indigo works, and of two thick-set waggoners,
we rescued those four gentlemen from their
sad situation, and condoled with them.

Not for £5 per head, however, would any
of our cabmen take them home; though a
man out of work had been tempted by a guinea,
to relieve them a little, with a long-handled
broom, and to flush them with a bucket, afterwards. Under heavy discouragement, they set
forth on their several ways, surveyed by the
police at a respectful distance, on account of
the danger to the public health.

CHAPTER V.

" GRIP."

My mother was so frightened, at the fright I had been through, that she took it for an urgent sign from Heaven, that my education should be stopped at once. Having had as much of school as I desired, I heartily hoped, that her opinion would prevail; but father was as obstinate as ever, and after the usual argument—in which she had the best of the words perhaps, and he of the meaning—I was bound to the altar of the Muses once again, with a promise of stripes, if I should try to slip the cord. Dr. Rumbelow undertook, that no professor of anything harder than languages—unless it were Professor Mega-low—should come in, at any door of the *Parthe-neion*, without having tallow poured over him,

which he had found, from high Greek authority,
to be the right ointment for Neo-sophistæ. And
he said that my father must have been familiar
with the passage he referred to, and had thus
discomfited all the Pansophistæ, better than any
modern Deipnosophist could have done. But my
father said no; he had never even heard of the
gentleman, with the hard name to crack; and as
to them Prophesiers, they ought to have pro-
phesied what his clots was, before tumbling
into them. He ought to have an action of
trespass against them; and, but for the law,
he would do so.

To make it quite certain, that no man of
science should analyse, synthesise, generalise,
or in any way scientise me, I was now provided
with a guardian, intrepid of neologisms ten
yards long. The father of our Bill Chumps,
Mr. Chumps, the Purveyor of Meat, was the
owner of a dog, who was the father of a pup,
who was threatening, every day, to make mince-
meat of the author of his existence. The old
dog might have tackled him, Bill told me, or at
any rate could have shown a good turn-up, but

for having broken his best fighting-tooth, on the
spiked collar of the last mastiff he had slain.
Through this disability on the part of old *Fangs*,
he found his son *Grip* too many for him; yet
could not be brought to confess it, and abstain
from a battle, at every opportunity. These
encounters in no wise disturbed Mr. Chumps,
but became inconvenient to Mrs. Chumps, when
she heard the piano (which had cost £10, for
her daughter, Belinda, to learn her scales) upset,
and entirely demolished. If it had been possible to hang *Grip*, hanged he would have been
that very day; for the mistress had nursed
Fangs through his distemper, and never would
listen to a word against him. Whereas the
whole fault was upon the side of *Fangs*; of
which I am quite certain, from the character of
Grip, as it unfolded itself before me, when he
became my own dear dog.

Providentially, their attempt to hang him had
proved a miserable failure. Not that he resisted
—he was too docile, and kind, and intelligent,
to do that—but because his neck was much
too thick, and manifold, and his wind too good,

for any rope to be of much account to him.
And before they could try any other form of
murder, his master came home, and made
short work with them, knowing the superiority
of the dog. Now, that same evening, the day
being Monday, the very choice club, to which
he, and my father, and Mr. John Windsor belonged, as well as the largest potato-man at
King's Cross, and the owner of the Indigo-blue
concern, and the most eminent merchant in the
cat's meat line, and several other gentlemen of
equal distinction, held their bi-daily congress at
" *The Best End of the Scrag*," at the corner.

That night there was a very fine attendance ;
and my father, who had long been acknowledged
to be the wittiest man on our side of the road—
perhaps because he got no chance at home, to
say what came inside him—upon this occasion
was compelled, by the nature of some of the
smells he had gone through, to be at his best,
as he generally was, after not less than two
glasses and a half. And he told the adventure
of the four professors, not as a sad and deplor-
able thing, but rather as matter for merriment.

In such a light did he put it, that all the gentlemen laughed heartily, most of all Mr. John
Windsor, who knew, even better than my father
.did, the variety of organic substance, active in
that pit just then.

"There's things there," he said, "to my
living knowledge, that'll never come out of their
hair while they live. And those big Savage-
Johns always have long hair, and as fuzzy as a
cat stroked upward. Why, the very last Friday,
when I was a-cooling, a pair of them comes with
a brazen machine, and asked me, as quiet as a
statue, permission for to taste my follet oils. I
up with the wooden spoon, and offered them a
drop; but that was not their meaning. It was
som'at about som'at we gives off, according
to them philanderers. And I says—'Government inquiry, gents?' And they says—'No,
sir; but for purposes of science.' 'Tell me,'
says I, 'what the constitootion is of this here
clot,' and they said 'Composite organic' something; while my composites all was upon the
upper floor, and never a hurdy-gurdy allowed
inside. 'So much for science!' says I; 'Jim,

show these gentlemen out, by the back-alley
door.' And now that you come to discourse of
it, Bubbly, it strikes me they might have come
very likely, smelling up a side-wind for your ·
poor Tommy."

"I should hope they have had enough of
that," said father; "if they come any more,
I'll boil them down, and make 'Science-sauce
for the million.' How would you like, John, to
pay your money, and get no change out of it,
along of such a lot?"

"You mean the missus," Mr. Windsor asked
—"won't allow Thistledown, as my Jack calls
him, to go to old Rum's any more, suppose?
Afraid of the ladies, Mr. Upmore is."

"I'll tell you what to do," Mr. Chumps broke
in; "Upmore, you buy my young dog *Grip*.
I'd give him to you with all my heart, if it
wasn't for the bad luck of it; though he is
worth ten guineas of anybody's money, for he
comes of the best blood in England. Downright
House of Lords bull-dog he is; same as should be
chained to the pillars of the State, to keep them
Glads, and Rads, away. Just you put him in

charge of Thistledown—or whatever you call
that little yellow-haired chap, and I'll back *Grip*
against all the Science, that ever made a pint
contain a pot."

" What's the figure ? " my father asked,
knowing how generously all men talk, and that
Mr. Chumps' bull-dogs were a fashionable race.

" If you was to offer me more than a crown,"
replied Mr. Chumps, with his fist on the table ;
" I should say, ' Bubbly, he's no dog of yours,
because you desire to insult me.' But put you
down a crown, as between old friends, and before
this honourable company, I say, ' Bucephalus
Upmore, *Grip* is your dog.' Why so ? John
Windsor here knows why, and so does Harry
Peelings from King's Cross, and so does Bill
Blewitt, and Sandy Mewliver, and all this
honourable company. And so do you, Bubbly
Upmore, if you are the man I have taken you
for. Gentlemen, it is because Mr. Upmore has
told the best story I have sat and listened to,
ever since last election day ; he digged a pit for
his enemies in the gate, and they fell into it
themselves ; as well as because my son, Bill

Chumps, who will make his mark, mind you, if
you live to see it, has taken a liking to this
gentleman's son—Thistledown, or Bubble-blow,
or Up-goes-the-donkey—they've got at least fifty
names for him—and, in my humble opinion, he
must be protected from the outrages of all those
fellows, philo-this, and anti-that,—my son Bill
knows their names, and all about them—who
have made the world a deal too clever for a quiet
man's comfort."

These very simple and sensible words were
received with much knocking on the table ; and
my father put down his five-shilling piece, so
that all the other gentlemen had time to see it,
before they began talking, as the subject compelled them to do, of the merits of their chil·
dren, respectively, severally, and all together.
And they parted, in thorough good will, inasmuch as not anybody listened to anybody else.

My father's opinion, at the time, had been that
the warmth of Mr. Chumps' political and social
feelings (promoted by the comforts of the club)
had hurried him into a disregard of money,
which his friends should never lose a moment to

improve. But when the journeyman came over in the morning, on his way to the *Partheneion*, with *Grip* trotting chained at the tail of the cart, my father cried—

"What! Has Chumps no more conscience, than to impose upon a friend like this? I, who have known him all these years, to pay as good a crown-piece as was ever coined, for a one-eyed, nick-eared, hare-lipped, broken-tailed son of a [female dog] like that! Gristles, you go back, and tell your master, that you saw me put an ounce of lead through him."

My father strode in, to fetch his gun, which he kept well-charged in the clock-case now, for the sake of so many Professors; and *Grip*, for a surety, would have been dead, and boiling, in less than five minutes, except for his luck. His luck was that I, being under debate between my two parents, had slipped out of doors, being old enough now by experience to know, that they took the kindest view of me, when I was out of sight. And coming round the corner, to peep in at the window, just to see whether they had settled my concerns, there I saw this poor dog—

hideous they might call him—doubtfully glanc-
ing in every direction, dimly aware that the
world was against him, scenting the death of a
dog in the air. One of his eyes was out of
sight, and one of his ears was in need of a
sling, his tail (which had lately been cracked by
his father) hung limp in the dust with a pitiable
wag, and every hair on his body was turned the
wrong way. His self-respect had suffered a
tremendous blow, by the effort of mankind to
hang him yesterday, and by dragging at the tail
of a cart to-day; and as sure as dogs are dogs,
he was aware of the awful decision against him.

Gristles was a hard man, and would not say a
word, to comfort or to plead for him, having got
a little snap from him, a month.or two ago; so
he looked down over the back of the cart, and
whistled—"Pop goes the Weasel"—while the
poor dog implored him, with all his one eye full
of wistful enquiry, what harm he had done.

"All right, guv'nor," shouted Gristles, as my
father came forth with his big double-barrel; "my
mare will stand fire like a church. But mind
you, it ain't no good to shoot at his head, with

nothing no smaller than a dockyard cannon.
Have at his heart, where you sees him now a-pant-
ing ; but for God's sake, guv'nor, don't shoot me."

That fellow's cowardly cruelty made my father
relent, for his heart was kind ; and before he
could put up his gun again, I was lying upon
Grip, and hugging him. The unfortunate dog,
for his last resource, had appealed to the only
weak face he could find, and my own fright
enabled me to enter into his.

"You little fool, Tommy, get out of the way,"
my father shouted ; but I would not budge, and
Grip put his quivering tongue out, and licked
my cheek, and besought me with a little speech
of whine.

"Very well," said my father, being glad of an
excuse for a milder course, as his wrath went
down, and knowing that, if he did this thing,
Mr. Chumps would never look at him again,
which would cost him as much as £20 a year ;
"very well, Tommy, if you like the brute,
you shall have him, and I hope he will be
grateful to you. Gristles, here's half-a-crown
for you, and you need not tell your master

what I said—only that I seemed a little disappointed with the first appearance of the dog;
which is rather a good fault, you know, in a
dog who has got to keep off strangers; and
my compliments, and I begin to feel sure that
Grip will soon begin to grow upon us."

This prophecy was fulfilled right well, so far
as my mother and self were concerned, and
even my father grew fond of *Grip*, as soon as
he found what a wonder he was; but the dog,
while regarding him with deep respect, could
never forgive his own narrow escape, any more
than forget my timely aid; for his memory was
as tenacious as his teeth. On me the dog
fastened his strong heart at once, with an
attachment more than dogged, making the best
of whatever I did, expecting no credit for his
own good works, humbly and heartily wagging
his tail, for the mere hope of a kind word, or look.

And, after a little while, no one who knew him
—at least if he were any judge of a dog—could
consider him ugly, from a proper point of view,
and without any personal feeling. For his eye,
that had seemed to be gone, came back, so as

nearly to agree with the other one, yet working
enough, on its own account, to redouble his
power of expression ; while his tail (being oiled
and done up with bell-wire) returned to its
natural tendency ; and as for his ear of a gin-
gery yellow, the colour was so rich that it
wanted shading, and gained it by having a
division introduced. So that, on the whole, he
had succeeded, without any serious damage to
himself, in impressing the main principle of the
present age—that of parental submission to the
child.

Now, when I appeared at the *Parthencion*,
under convoy of this gallant animal, Dr. Rumbelow scarcely knew what to do. After looking
at *Grip*, with some surprise, he fired a strong
volley of quotations at him ; but the dog moved
never a tail-point for them, and instead of being
frightened, he would not even blink, but gazed
at them calmly ; as much as to say, " There is
not a pinch of shot in the whole of them."

The Doctor, though one of the bravest of mankind, could not return his gaze, with equal largeness and frank placidity of criticism, but shouted

for Mercury, his page, and bade him remember the glorious day whereon he slew the monster Argus. Bob Jackson, failing to recall that date, looked as if he would rather keep aloof from *Grip*, who opened his nostrils, and curled up his lips, and shot fire out of his discordant eyes.

"Good doggie, good doggie,—poor fellow"— said the page, in a tenderly condescending tone, while approaching sideways gingerly; "if he is a very good doggie, he shall have this beautiful collar to wear,—oh lor ! "

He was lying on his back, with *Grip* standing across him, but scarcely thinking it worth while to bite him, unless he should endeavour to make escape. "Fetch me the big cane, labelled No. 1," the Doctor shouted valiantly, "the father of all canes, the *rhopalos*, which has warmed the back of a prime-minister. With that will I rescue my Hermes, though the Hydra herself stand over him."

"No, sir ; no, sir ; for God's sake don't go near him," cried Bill Chumps, running up the play-ground ; " *Grip* can beat any two men in

the world, because no blow can hurt him.
Leave him to me, sir; I understand him, and
he knows me well enough, though he never
took to me, somehow or other, as his dear old
father does. He has taken wonderfully to Fly
Tommy. Somebody come, and give Tommy a
good whack."

Of the many brave boys, who had rejoiced in
doing this, even without instigation last week,
there was not one who would now discharge this
duty, for the public weal. "Why should I hit
him?" said boy after boy, who said last week,
"Why shouldn't I?"—"I am a deal too fond of
poor Tommy for that. Hit him yourself, if you
want him hit."

"So I will, then, you pack of dirty cowards,"
answered Chumps, being put upon his mettle,
though he told me afterwards that he was in
a horrid funk; and he gave me at once a good
sounding smack, on a part of my body that was
covered with material warranted to wear, and
having three stout seams with a piece to let out.
Before the echo of the Five's court ceased, *Grip*
was between us, looking up at me, as if to ask,

"What am I to do?" doubting in his mind whether justice would allow him to wage war against his late master's son.

"Worthy is he to be piled with praise—not *cumulari*, but *qui cumuletur*, boys of the second form observe—inasmuch as he has not doubted to encounter, singly, or in maniple, all the foes of the pusill committed to his charge. Great is the manhood of this dog; and yet it somewhat repenteth me that, provoked by the wanton assaults of science upon the sweet retirement of the Muses, I have promised him the tub, and the collar, and the bowl, of the deceased, and perhaps now constellated animal, Heracles Poikilostiktos. Mercury, brush thy pulverulent *petasus*, and with the aid of thy lyre, or that of the ever ready-minded Chumps, conduct this formidable animal to the many-strewn couch prepared for him. *Partheneionidæ*, the hour has struck. With grateful ardour, let us hasten to the banquet of the mind provided for us, by the generous wisdom of the men of old."

With these words, our great master strode to the school-room door; and we (his children and the fruit of his cane) looked vainly for chance of escape from work. Then, with as much of a sigh as childhood yet has learned from nature's book, we followed the learned steps afar, with two for one in length, but only one for two in speed, I ween.

CHAPTER VI.

TRUE SCIENCE.

For some years now, I had a quiet time, increasing in knowledge very gradually, but as fast as my teachers thought needful. For the only true way to get on in learning, is not to be in too much of a hurry, counting every step, and losing breath, and panting into violence of perspiration; but rather to take, as the will of the Lord, whatever gets carried into us, allowing it to settle, and breed inside, with the help of imagination. Under the steadfast care of *Grip*, and furtherance of Dr. Rumbelow, I advanced pretty fairly in fine acquirements, which have proved, once or twice, to be serviceable.

To me, and to all the school, and indeed a considerable number of the houses around, it

was a sad and bitter day, when William
Chumps, Esquire—for that was his proper style
now, under stamp (as he showed us) of several
letters—was at last compelled to say farewell
to the *Partheneion*, and the whole of us. He
had been elected to a scholarship, founded for
that purpose by his father at the *Partheneion*,
to the amount of five shillings a week for three
years, as a tribute to humane letters, and the
many good contracts for meat Mr. Chumps had
performed. And Bill was to take it to Oxford,
and perhaps when the " Chumps Scholarship "
became talked about, obtain some good orders
to supply his college; for a great deal of meat is
consumed in Hall.

" Tommy," said Bill, the very day he was to
leave, when he saw me crying about his departure, for he always had been so good to me,
" keep up your spirits, young fellow, and don't
blub. The fault of your nature is, being so soft.
Now, why am I going to the grandest old place,
and the finest young fellows, on the face of the
earth? Simply because I have got so much
pluck. I am not such a wonderfully clever

cove, though everybody seems to think so; and I have plenty to learn yet, I can assure you. And of course I know well enough, that I am going among big swells, who have a right to be swells, not snobs from the Poultry, and Mincing Lane, such as used to try to snub me here. But do you think I have a particle of funk? Feel the muscle in my arm, Tommy."

"Bill," I replied, "you could knock them all down; but when you had done it, there would be fifty more."

"Tommy, my boy, I will not hurt one of them, unless he endeavours to cock over me. If it comes to any fighting, at my time of life, it must be done with pistols. But my mind is made up, not to meddle with any man, unless he insults me, and then let him look out. They will very soon discover that I mean to be a gentleman, although my father may be called a butcher; and when they see that, if they are gentlemen themselves, they will be very glad to show me the way. The great defect of your character, Tommy, is that you have not got go enough."

"I should think I have heard enough of that,"

I said; "just because I don't want to fly, to please you chaps that cock over me."

"You are putting the cart before the horse," replied Chumps, having taken already six lessons in logic, from a man who came on purpose; "you have an extraordinary gift of flying, which would make your fortune, Tommy, and enable your father to leave off poisoning the public, if only you would cultivate it. I can do very good Latin Elegiacs, and tidy Greek Iambics, and run a mile in four minutes and three-quarters; but how many years might I hammer at all that, and scarcely turn a sixpence? But you—you have only to put on your wings, and astonish all the North of London. If I had only got your turn for flying, with my own for the classics, and for going to the top, I tell you what it is, Tommy Upmore—in ten years I'd be the Prime Minister of England."

My own opinion was, that without any flying, Bill would arrive at the top of the tree, in about five years, which was a long time yet for any one to look forward to; and thinking so much of him now, and grieving so deeply for the loss of him,

I allowed his words to sink into my mind, as
they never had done before. Hitherto I had
been inclined to think, if ever I thought about it,
that my want of proper adhesion to the ground
was a plague to me, and no benefit. My father
treated it as a thing to laugh at, and to dis-
believe in; my mother was afraid that I never
might come down, within her reach, and the same
as I went up; while the rest of the world was
content to take it entirely from a selfish point
of view, as a question of science, or of low
curiosity.

But before we could say any more about that,
"old Rum," as we called him, came into the
hall, where Chumps was waiting with his boxes,
for his father's meat-van to fetch them. The
doctor had already said farewell to Bill, before
all the school, and as a public essay; but now
he came to say good-bye, and to give him a
few kind words, with a friendly heart. Bill was
as tall as his master now, being an exceedingly
strapping fellow, and thoroughly thriven on
the marrow of the ox; but when the Doctor
took his hand, and spoke to him in a low,

soft voice, without any Latin turn in it, the cup
of Bill's feelings began to run over, and I ran
away, not to look at it.

Here in a passage, as facts would have it, with
my eyes full of tears and shadow, I ran into the
arms, or legs, of a strong, hard man. Hard in
the matter of bones, I mean, and the absence
of any fat about him, but as soft and tender
in heart, and vein, as anything he had ever
dissected.

"Why, Tommy! It is indeed our Tommy!"
exclaimed Professor Megalow. "Prolepsis of
our race, what trouble is upon you?"

"Oh, sir," cried I, "if you could only stop Bill
Chumps from going away from us! The place
will be nothing, after he is gone, and nobody will
want to stop here. Whatever you order is sure
to be done."

"Well," said the Professor, as he lifted me
up, and looked at me kindly with his large, calm
eyes, "I have come a long way to make that
discovery; and I wish it were so in Great
Russell Street."

He was thinking of his labours, and forgetting

a far more important matter in our eyes—the
two half-holidays procured for us, when he
thought that we seemed to require them. For
now his vast knowledge, and accuracy, simplicity, gentleness, and playful humour, had won
the warm friendship of our Dr. Rumbelow, who
seldom caned any of us now, except for lying.
For my part, I loved this kind gentleman, and
grieved that he had not once asked me to fly for
him.

"My friend, you are often in my thoughts,"
he said, as if he knew all that was passing in
my mind; "let us sit down awhile in this quiet
corner, and consider a highly scientific case,
which happens to be in my pocket."

Smiling at the fright his words had caused,
he drew forth a pretty little globular box, yellow,
pellucid, and inlaid with stars of gold; and this
he held so that the light of the sun glanced
through it, illuminating things inside, that
danced with colour, purple, and orange, and
rosy red. I pulled out my handkerchief, and
dried my eyes, and pushed back my curls, for
a hearty good stare.

"Tommy, your mind is of a wholesome type," said the great Professor pleasantly; "brief should be the pangs of youthful woe. And they are all good to eat, Tommy; and as you suck them, you can pull them out of your mouth, and see the sun shine through, and then put them back, and find them ever so much sweeter."

"Oh, but I can't get at them, sir! What good can they be, if I can't get at them?"

"Your reasoning is wonderfully sound and good, from its own point of view," he answered. "But get at them, Tommy, and they shall be yours; you shall have box and all, if you open it."

This was very hard upon me; for I had no more chance of opening it, than of flying in the air, as people say, and indeed, according to my gifts, much less. In vain I pulled, and squeezed, and pressed, examined every part of it, and then worked away again, screwing up my lips, and eyes, so sternly that the Professor could not help laughing. And the worst of it was, that the more I laboured, the greater the temptation of the inside grew, everything dancing with a play of colours glorious to see, and feel that all was good to eat.

"Oh, sir, I can't, I can't get at them ; do please to show me the way, sir," I cried ; for truly it was enough to make me cry.

" My boy," said the Professor, looking gravely at me, and seeming to wink with one large clear eye, though it was not a wink, but rather the effect of a most sagacious and delightful nod; "I have long anticipated that result. It is always agreeable to find one's prognosis confirmed by events, though they often fail to do it. No one has found out the secret of this box, though very clever men have striven at it, and among them three noted puzzle-makers. Perfect simplicity is deeper than any depth of complexity. Tommy, behold, and with good will devour. Ha, a practical, rather than a theoretic mind ! "

Perhaps he made that observation because, without stopping to ask how the box came open, I fell to at once upon its choice contents. The flavour was altogether new to me, and wonderfully fine and penetrating, leaving no part of

the mouth in idleness, and warming the entire
length of throat with hope. At the same time,
these goodies had just enough about them of
roughness, to compel the tongue to stop, and
invite it to dwell upon their surface gently,
equably, earnestly, and with much delight
refraining from speech, while thus better employed.

"Ah!" said the Professor, and one "ah" of
his contained all the fulness of three volumes;
"Tommy, be just, and consider them fairly.
They are made from my own design, and
stamped with cuneiform—ah, I see it now!
The young mind is plagued so with ancient
tongues, that the young tongue rejoices in
demolishing their symbols. By taking a patent
for this design, I might get on better than by
building dragons. But let us return to our
point, my good Tommy."

As he spoke, he was setting against one
another the tips of his long middle fingers,
which I took for the point to be returned to, and
said, "Yes, sir, if you please, sir."

"My young friend, I take it that the point,

from which we have allowed our minds to be
pleasantly diverted, is whether you will allow
me just to give you a lift in the air—a very gentle
lift ; not for any scientific view whatever, but
only for a little satisfaction to myself. If from
old experience of professors, you have any mis-
giving, say so, Tommy, and I will not touch you."

"Oh, sir," said I, with my mouth running
over ; "don't be afraid, sir, to lift me where
you like."

At this good encouragement, Professor Megalow nodded, as if in pleasant commune with
himself ; and then with one hand softly tossed
me to his shoulder, where I sate very nicely, as
on a spring-cushion, rather than a feather-bed,
however. Then he handed me up the box,
which I put between my knees, and began to
sing, according to my habit, when contented
with the world.

"Ah," said the Professor, as he walked about
(having, now and then, a little whistle to himself), and took me to look at a map of mountains
(placed at a mountainous height above my usual
level of intelligence), "Tommy, this is very

good; this is quite delightful. Do you know, why this is so delightful, little Tommy?"

"Yes, sir," I replied, for I was very clever then; "it is jolly, because they are so capital to suck."

"Not only that, Tommy; although I am perfectly open to conviction upon that point"—here he opened his mouth. and I popped a goody in, as if he were the boy, and I the celebrated man —"but also because, my most generous young friend, it confirms my opinion, or, in finer words, my theory. Most of us, as we get older and older, grow more and more interested in ourselves. Possibly you are too young, small Tommy, to have any desire as yet to hear an empeirical, rather than a scientific opinion, about your peculiar, but not altogether unparalleled, case."

"If you please, sir, to say anything you like. And I won't be afraid, and I won't tell my mother. unless you are sure that you would not be afraid. And if you talk as plainly as you did just now, I will try to make out what the meaning is."

Professor Megalow put me down, with a gentle clap on my back, as if he had found me one too much for him. And then, with a jerk of his prominent chin, and a rub of his nose, he considered me.

And while he was doing all this, such a smile of large good-will illumined us, that I would have been glad to be dissected, if it would please him, and not hurt much.

The only thing that saddened me was this— he did not appear to be at all astonished, by anything discovered in me. And I now called to mind, that he never had shown any special excitement about my case, as all the other scientific men had done. And my mother had said that he could not be half so clever as his reputation was, because of his letting me alone so. Though perhaps he was paid by the year for his work, and the others by the job ; which would account for everything. That may have been so, and I thought about it now, and concluded (from brief observation of his hat) that he only got his money at the end of the year.

"The difference," said the Professor calmly,

with a glance of affection at his large-skulled hat, which was rolling on the floor without taking any harm, " according to my very humble opinion, is not so much of kind as of degree, my Tommy. It has long been well known that the various families of the human race—as we may venture still to call it—differ very greatly in specific gravity; the Celt, for instance, is especially heavy in proportion to his size, and the Jute the opposite. There was, I believe, an exceptionally light and buoyant race in North America, aboriginal so far as we know; and the lightest member of that race, Tommy, would probably have despised your highest flight. At the same time, and although I have met with a case of almost equal levity—the example being, I regret to say, feminine—you must not imagine that I am endeavouring to disparage your exploits, my dear Tommy. Don't cry, my dear child; I had no idea that you were so sensitive upon this matter. Your admirable master has always told me, that your main desire is to stop upon the ground, and that both your parents wish it. You nod your head, as if I understood your feelings. Then why are your blue eyes full of tears ? "

" If you please, sir, I wasn't at all longing to go up. Only I didn't know anybody else had done it. And I shan't care to go up any more, after that."

" Well ! " cried the Professor, with his great rich smile; " human nature has no exceptions half so wonderful as its laws are. My good little friend, allow me to comfort you, and to restore your self-respect. It is not by any means a common thing for members of the English race to fly—excuse me for using the popular, but incorrect word, to describe your exploits. But there is a power that beats you, Tommy, in your own province, and that is Time. At three o'clock I have a lecture to deliver upon your antitype, the apteryx, a bird that has abdicated the rights, which some of us desire to usurp."

" Oh, sir, do let me come and hear it, if old Rum will let me go. Bill Chumps has heard you lecture, and he says—— "

" I thank him heartily for his approval ; "

replied the Professor, at the same time showing
me his watch, which ticked with a bullet upon
cat-gut; " William Chumps is a fine young man,
with a great spirit in a strong body; and I
would ask your kind master to let you come, if
I thought the subject good for you. But, my
dear little fellow, I am sure that it is not so.
The less your mind runs upon the regions of
the air, and the more you endeavour to bring
your body, by good feeding, exercise, pleasant
sports, and moderate labours, to the normal
specific gravity, the better it will be for yourself,
and your parents, whose only child you are.
And I venture to differ from my learned
brethren, Professors Brachipod, and Jargoon,
Chocolous, and Mullicles, in thinking that it
will' be no worse for the interests of science.
Good-bye, Tommy; you may keep the box, as a
souvenir of this long interview; be sure that
you eat all you can of good meat, solid bread,
and glutinous material; and don't swallow too
much Latin and Greek, which tend to undue
elation. If you were a lazy boy, I should not
tell you this; but I hear that you are an

ambitious boy, and eager to learn everything. I shall observe you, my interesting friend, and from time to time hint to your learned master any trifle that escapes the unmedical mind."

He lifted me up, and kissed my forehead; and as I picked up his hat—a trifle which had escaped his universal mind—and by jumping on a chair clapped it on his mighty head, I could not help paying him the usual tribute paid at his departure—glistening eyes, that is to say, and a smile of loving wonder.

CHAPTER VII.

THE GREAT WASHED.

My father, Bucephalus Upmore, had been, at
the time of my birth, a Radical, and owed his
conversion from loose ideas to no amount of
argument, or even of wider observation, but to
a little accident. Upon his return, one winter
night, from a meeting in St. Pancras, not only
of a liberal, but a wildly generous character,
somebody tripped him up, and stole his watch,
and purse, and Sunday hat. A small man
might have accepted this as a lesson against
subversive views, and a smaller one as a con-
firmation of them; but my father was not of
that sort. His practice was, to take his stand
upon what he considered right, and allow no
evidence to move him one hair's breadth from

the true conclusions poured into him. And he never read anything, that did not cap and sawder down his own contents.

This had made his life thus far most happy, enabling him to despise all people who differed in any way from him, as well as to enlarge himself, without any compulsion to pay for it. And he might have gone on in this easy way, calling upon the people behind him to rob the people in front of him, if he had not undergone the bad luck to be robbed himself. When he came to speak of this, among his friends, not one of them failed to express deep sorrow, and to assure him that such things must happen, whenever the Conservatives were in office. At the same time they intimated gently, that when he made so much money out of working men, it served him right to lose some of it.

His feelings were hurt by this sometimes; especially when the suggestion came from gentlemen, who had attained that degree, by adulterating the victuals of the working man. However, he smothered his common sense, as the first duty is of Liberals; till his body and

mind came thump upon a stumbling-block, and
no mistake.

Arising in a vast hall of Reform, to second a
motion that all men are equal, and must have
the same money for their work (whether they do
it, or leave it undone), and must not do more than
six hours in a day—for fear of imparting infection
to the rest—with his mouth full of reason, and his
heart full of hope [that none of his men might
be there to hear him], my dear father gave a
stamp, and found it fall upon something soft
and dull. He felt himself more at home through
this, having so much soft stuff round his vats,
and his eloquence mounted to full swell, till he
wanted to jump to give emphasis. This he
attempted to do with a clap of his hands, to
complete a grand sentence, when up came something between his legs, and got stuck on the
top of his highlows. With laudable agility, my
father stooped, while the audience cheered
lustily, supposing him to be in quest of some
word big enough to express his sentiments.

These, however, demanded outlet, in a very
short one, when he found in his hand his own lost

hat, with a hole in the brim from the stamp of his heel, and the crown chock-full of heads for speech, and demolitionist statistics. He examined his hat, and descried B. U. just in under the tuck of the lining, where a Liberal always puts his mark, on the Vote-by-ballot principle.

This alone was enough to shake his confidence in his party; though all the gentlemen around him looked quite incapable of doing anything. And he might, as he said to my mother, have believed that his old hat had come down from heaven, if only his new hat, bought last Friday, had been left for him to go home with. That, however, was not the case; his new hat managed to leave that great assembly upon the head of some eminent Liberal; and my father went home with his old hat on, greasy, and dirty, and showing signs of conflict, but containing a head that would be Radical no more.

Now, I need not have told that little story— which repeats itself among such people, more often than it is repeated—except to explain what it was that took us, in the summer holidays, to a place called "Happystowe-on-Sea."

It appears that my father was by no means
satisfied so to lose his hats—though in truth it
was no great grievance, thus to save the contents
at the cost of the case—and like a thorough
Briton, as he always was, he determined not to
get the worst of it. Several opportunities for
reprisal had been allowed to escape him ; when,
soon after Bill Chumps went to Oxford, there
came among us, and excited our principles, a
contested election for Marylebone. By means
of their noble organization, the Liberals knew,
from the outset, that the battle of freedom was
sure to be won ; or, as our people put it, rank
bribery and corruption, truckling and swilling
would defeat the right. Nevertheless, a just
hope was entertained, on both sides, of a very
lively contest, and a fair occasion (without legal
intervention) for sounding the capacity of an
adversary's head. My father was flying a big
blue flag, which we could see from the *Parthencion*, with " Church and State for ever " on
it ; and Mr. John Windsor, and Chumps
Esquire—as we called the great butcher in
respect of his son—and " *The Best End of the*

Scrag," all had the same ; and only a man who
knocked horses on the head durst hang out the
red rag, up our Lane.

I speak of this, only as a circumstance to
prove that our neighbourhood was Constitutional,
and that the Radical element, however respectable it might have been when kept at home, had
no right whatever to come invading us, and desiring to trample on our principles. They knew
that for nearly three hundred and fifty yards, the
inhabitants were all true-Blue, beginning with
the Indigo factory on the South, and going all
through the ash-heaps, and ending with my
father. But in the wantonness of triumph,
when their majority was posted up 2,000
[though our side claimed 1,500 in front] these
" Demi-Cats "—as Bill had sent us word from
Oxford to entitle them, and so we did—must
needs assemble at King's Cross, in their thousands, and resolve to storm every Blue house in
Maiden Lane.

The beginning of their enterprise was most
glorious ; nothing could stand before them.
They broke all the glass that had a blue flag

near it, and they knocked down every man who
had got blue eyes. The premises of Mr.
Chumps were sacked; his legs of mutton walked
off, as if they were alive, and his salt beef was
stuck on poles, even bigger than the skewers he
weighed it out with; every drop in the cellars of
the Conservative Hotel ran uphill inside a big
Radical, and Mr. John Windsor lost soap
enough pretty nearly to clean half the Liberals.
However, he contrived to get over a back wall,
together with his wife and daughter Polly—Jack
was luckily at the *Parthencion*, and the other
four gone to see their Aunt, with old *Fangs* to
protect them from the Liberals—and by taking
an in-and-out way through the cinders, the
three arrived safely at our back door, without
breath enough to blow out one of their own dips.

Till now my father had scarcely struck a blow
on behalf of the Constitution, beyond giving
his vote, and knocking down a man who was
anxious to do the like to him; but now it did
seem a bit too hard that the Liberals should
extinguish thus all liberty of opinion.

"John," he said now, as he brought in the

fugitives, and heard a tremendous noise coming
up the Lane, "this is what I call coming it too
strong. Mrs. Windsor, ma'am, you are all of a
tremble. Sophy, get whiskey and water, at once."

"Bubbly," poor Mr. Windsor gasped, "this
is most kind, and cordial of you. My dear, you
require a stimulant, however much you dislike it.
But, Upmore, down with your flag, at once!
Down with your flag, that the fellows may go by."

"Oh yes, Mr. Upmore," implored Mrs.
Windsor, a lady of a most superior kind;
"please not to lose a moment in hauling down
your flag; it is flying in the face of Providence.
Do cut the ropes, if it won't untie."

"Will I?" said my father, and his face took
on, as my mother said afterwards, a very fine
expression; "lower my flag, to the scum of the
earth! Ladies, go down to the cellar, and keep
quiet. You will have no one here, while my flag
is flying. Mr. Windsor is a man of high spirit,
as he has proved many times, in our debates.
He, and I, will go to the boiling-house, and
defend the true-blue, come what will."

My mother declares that Mr. Windsor was

going, at his best pace, to the cellar-stairs, when
she locked him out, and pulled out the key; but
mother was always severe upon him, because of
his wholesale ways, and talk. At any rate, he
did not flag or fly, although he may have longed
to do so perhaps.

"Now, John," said my father, as he took his
arm, to confirm his courage (which required it),
and led him down the red-tiled passage to the
boiling-house; "you have had a great many
good laughs at my little steam-engine, haven't
you? Very well, we'll try it on the 'Great
unwashed;' if there happens to be a bit of fire
left. My men are all away, the same as yours
—or else these fellows would not come to sack
us. I gave them the quarter-day to vote, the
same as you did with yours; and mine are gone
the right colour to a man, I do believe. But I
happened to say, 'leave a little steam on;' and
I can get up a great deal in ten minutes, and
the blackguards won't be here for twenty.
They've got three blue houses yet to wreck, and
my double-gates will keep them out, at least five
minutes."

" I see, I see, what you mean to do. What a glorious fellow you are, Bubbly! I'll go half the waste of phleg."

" Then go and see that all the bolts are right, while I get up steam, and have the double hose ready."

These two gallant, and sturdy, boilers very soon had the front and back gates barred and bolted, and strengthened with struts against the styles; so that all the men who could get at them must take at least five minutes to get through them; and meanwhile the furnace of the little engine was beginning to roar, and the steam to puff.

" Capital! I call this first-rate stoking;" exclaimed my father, as he stopped to breathe. " Now you understand the hose, John? It is only three-inch pipe, and therefore as handy as a walking-stick. You put your nozzle upon that trestle, commanding the back doors, while I keep ready for the time they have broken the front gate down. We have got a big vat of hot stuff to draw from; but I don't think they'll want half of it."

"Bubbly, I don't seem to understand it," said Mr. Windsor, who was slow-headed, and losing his presence of mind, perhaps (although he had got his coat off) from working so hard while he was fat, and with terrible Liberal screeches already arising in the air, above the rattle of the gates; "suppose, my dear friend, that we killed some fellow!"

"No hope of that," said my father, being now in a rancorous, and determined frame; "I am afraid that the temperature won't be above 160°, if so much; and it cools in passing through the air too fast. It will only make their eyes sharp, and their faces clean, as they should be on a holiday. No white feather, John Windsor, now! Ah, they've fetched the blacksmith, as I knew they would. Think of your wife and children, John, and of the British Constitution. Things must be come to a very pretty pass, if a man mayn't syringe a born jackass! Especially when the jackass kicks his gate in."

"In for a penny, then, in for a pound," his brother boiler answered, with his courage up;

" whatever you order shall be done, friend Bubbly. This vat shall run away, before I do."

" I'll go bail for the front gate, Johnny, if you'll be ready for the rear attack, supposing they've the cheek to try one. This engine works a double hose, you see, on the principle of a well-coil. Now, my fine fellows, what do you want here ? "

The blacksmith, though working against his will—for my father always paid him ready money—had prized one heavy gate off its hinges, and the other was swagging to fall with it.

" We wants you, guv'nor, and your scurvy flag ; " cried the leader of the mob, a chimney-sweep.

" B'iler, b'iler ; we wants the Tory b'iler ! " cried a hundred dirty fellows, as the gates crashed in.

" Well, and you shall have him," said my father, who was standing just outside the slow-house door, with the nozzle of the hose tucked under his arm, and a rod in his right hand to put the pressure on ; " if you come a yard further, you shall taste the boiler. Only let

blacksmith Grimes get out of the way. I
don't wish to boil a respectable neighbour.
And I don't want to boil you, unless you insist
on it."

Not only Grimes, but a great many others
would have liked to get out of the way at this;
but the bulk of the tumult behind shoved on,
and the heads, that were fain to hang back, got
jammed up in front against the smash, and
then shot over. Father just waited, till the
chimney-sweep, a termagant of the highest rank,
was hurra-ing, and waving a soot-brush,—and
then he let go hot candles at them. In a long
white column, flew the scalding fluid, spreading,
like a sheaf, when it met their faces, and coat-
ing every man of them with poisonous gray
froth. No man could swear, for his mouth was
bunged up; and no man could strike, for his
arms were stuck to him, with a weight of
deposit, like a stalactite. Good stearine it
was, of the value of at least three halfpence a
pound, in the unrefined state; and it went
inside their shirts, and stung like hornets, and
settled into every cracked place of the skin,

and made a man tight in his linings. And to
add to their grief, such a steam arose among
them—not to mention something else beginning
with same letters—that the slits of any eyes,
that were left half open, were as useless as in a
thick London fog.

" There's a deal more to come," said my father
calmly; " noble reformers, stand shoulder to
shoulder; as one of your writers has beautifully
said—the deeper we go, the more strength we get."

The issue is told in a ballad written that
same night at " *The Best End of the Scrag*;"
which,—though inspired by Liberal ale, for
" *The Scrag* " had not a drop left of its own, and
was obliged to send across the road for it—is
a poem of high merit; and my father was told
upon the best authority that the poet, from
first to last, received nearly fifteen shillings for
it. Our house subscribed for sixpenceworth,
and so did Mr. Windsor; and all the boys of
the lower order, up to Grotto-day, were singing
—no matter what their politics might be—and
wrapping their bulls' eyes up in, " The lay of
the soporific soap-boilers." The Radicals bore

this satire well, having had their own way in
everything, and laughed on the right side of
their mouths; and even the men, who had been
cased in grease, made a good thing of it, when
they scraped themselves, by going to the rag-
and-bone-shops. Yet, as bad luck would have
it, the leading mind among them—that of Mr.
Joe Cowl, the Master-sweep—was not content,
and broke out into a summons at the Clerken-
well Police Court. For Mr. Cowl, meeting all
the first of the discharges, before the stearine
was well up in the hose, was a loser instead
of a receiver of deposit. All the soot on his
body was clean washed off; and nothing being
left to fill the pores, the abnormal exposure
of his system led to a pungent, pervasive, and
radical catarrh. Mrs. Cowl sent for a doctor,
but her husband Joe had still enough vitality to
kick him out; and then jumping from the frying-
pan into the fire, shouted loudly for a lawyer;
and he recommended law.

CHAPTER VIII.

FOR CHANGE OF AIR.

" But," said my father to Mr. John Windsor, who was urging him to leave home for a while, that Joe Cowl's anger might blow over ; " people pretend not to understand it, John ; but you know as well as I do what it is. How could I ever live, for a fortnight at a stretch, or even three weeks, as might be needful, without a breath of the air of the works, John ? "

" When I was obliged to spend a week in Parree," replied Mr. Windsor (who, as Mrs. Windsor said, had " acclimatised himself uncommon quick to the French style, and their accent "), " I thought I should have died for a day or two, from the downright emptiness of the air. But, my dear fellow, I found out some

places, where the air was as nourishing, every
bit, as it is at our works on an over-time day.
Bubbly, I contrived to bilk the doctor, by going
twice a day to a place with a hole in it, over
some large cookery vapours. And you must
contrive to find a place like that. I'll tell you
what, go away to the seaside. At the seaside
now, they are always making smells."

" So they are, I am sure," said Mrs. Windsor,
who was come to join in the attack on father;
" the last time I was at Brighton, my dear, with
all the poor children, how I envied you, dwelling,
—as the poet so graphically describes it,—in
the sweet fragrancy of home. Mr. Upmore, the
air is never empty at any fashionable seaside
place; and for the sake of your dear wife, and
your wonderfully interesting boy, who is a dear
friend of my clever Johnny's, you cannot, with
any consistency whatever, refuse to respond to
the call of duty; for duty it is, and should be
looked at in that light, without a second thought
of paltry money."

" She has the gift of eloquence," declared her
husband; " and sometimes I almost wish she

hadn't. It comes to her from her mother's side,
whose mother was a celebrated Baptist preacher.
And when it is upon her, she has no consideration of other people's money, and not so very
much of mine. But you must not take the
whole of this for high talk, Bubbly. To make
yourself scarce just now, will fetch you a pound,
for every penny you have to spend. An old
friend of mine is well up the back-stairs; and
although he could never do a stroke for me—for
some reason, which he explains much better than
I can understand it—he whispered to me, last
night, 'keep in with the gentleman, who boils
higher up the Lane than you do. His fortune is
made, if he keeps quiet, and the present Government remains in office. He will have more jobs
than he can do, and he must call you in, to help
him.' I thought I had better tell you, Bubbly;
because we have always been straight-forward;
and if you are pulled up in the Police-court, why,
you might have to wait months, before you got
a contract."

My father stood up, for nothing could be more
illustrative of true friendship, more incentive to

patriotism, and more ennobling to the human race, than this announcement from his brother boiler. He had passed through a good deal of emotion lately, having been not only toasted largely, wherever he appeared with his purse in his pocket, and visited with post-cards more than once (from people whose names were in the papers) but even invited to a hot dinner, which he took care to go to, at the Mansion-House. For that Lord-Mayor was not one of those, who desire to have no successor.

"John Windsor, we have always been straight-forward. There has never been the shadow of a doubt between us. Our friendship has never known a cloud upon it;" I was home for the holidays now, and these words of my father's made me stare a little; "you know what I am, John,—a humble Briton, who thinks for himself, and sticks to it. Business is business; politics come in the evening, to smoke a pipe with. When I was a lad, I may have thought of making something out of it. But I only made a loss of two good hats."

"Hear, hear!" interrupted Mr. Windsor;

"and now by repulse of the Rads, you have gained three hundred hats, the poet says."

"Stuff!" cried my father; "there were not thirty; and shocking bad hats all of them. You are welcome to your share, if you will take your half of this confounded summons, Windsor."

"Gentlemen, come," said Mrs. Windsor, "if you once begin with politics—the point is to settle where to go to, and I think Mrs. Upmore should have a voice in that. What coast do you prefer, my dear?"

"My views are of very little moment," mother answered quietly, as she came in, with a bottle of cherry-brandy in her hand; "Bucephalus is so bigoted. But I love to see the sun rise over the sea from the window, and then go to bed again."

"Your taste, ma'am, is of the very highest order," said Mr. Windsor, who never could persuade his wife to turn her hand to pickles, and bottled fruit, and gravies; "and many a time have I enjoyed the fine results that comes of it. To see the sun rise over the sea, and the poor

fellows shaking about in their boats, and then
to go to bed again, while they are catching
fish enough for your breakfast, prawns, and
lobsters, and a sole with egg and bread-crumbs,
and perhaps (if they are lucky) just a salmon-
collop—ah, that is what I call seaside! And
then, you lounge about, and see fine ladies jumping up and down, as the white waves knock
them ; and then you have a pipe, and smell fine
smells, and talk to an old salt, as if you were
his captain; and he shows you, through his spy-
glass, how rough it is outside, with the people
in the vessels looking enviously at you ; and by
that time, Bubbly, why you want your dinner ;
and you eat it, as if you was made for nothing
else."

"I don't remember much about it," answered
father, though evidently struck by this description ; "why, it must be thirty years since I saw
the sea. Ah, how we go up and down in life!
I dare say I was no bigger than that little
shrimp there."

"Mr. Upmore!" exclaimed Mrs. Windsor,
whose manner, we were told, was more aristo-

cratic than anything on our side of King's
Cross; "Mr. Upmore, with all your opportunities, is it possible that you have not ever
felt it your very first duty, to take your dear
wife, and your Tommy, to the sea? Whatever
should we do, without the sea? A great part
of our commerce comes over it, and my Johnny
can very nearly swim! Dear Mrs. Upmore, you
should not lose a minute, in taking your darling
boy to the sea. It seems to be considered so
essential now, that all young persons should be
taught to swim."

"My Tommy can fly, ma'am," replied dear
mother; "and what is swimming to compare
with that?"

"I'll tell you what," said Mr. Windsor, "if
you want to see the sun rise over the sea, the
best chance for it is on the east coast. I'm
very partial to Brighton myself, not being so
exclusive as Mrs. W. about a little smell here,
or a sort of odour there. That feeling of the
higher orders seems to be cutaneous."

"Spontaneous, you mean, Mr. Windsor, or
perhaps contagious, or indigenous."

"I mean what I say, my dear. And what I say is this—to the best of my knowledge, the sun don't get up out of the sea, at Brighton, though he does come over it, in fine weather, by the time the upper classes are looking about. But I won't pretend to speak positive, because I never got up to look for him. Only this I do say, and it stands to reason,—if you want to compel him to get up there, you had better go where the sea runs east."

"To be sure, I see!" my father answered: "I am not sure, that I should have thought of that. John, you are a clever fellow, after all."

"I should hope that he was;" cried Mrs. Windsor; "because you have made yourself famous, Mr. Upmore, with my husband to stand in front of you, are you going to begin to look down upon us?"

"Don't be so hot, my dear. I assure you, Bubbly, that she means it for the moment; but it goes in two seconds, like a spurt of steam. Now, I happen to know a very nice little place, on the east coast, Norfolk or Suffolk, I believe, for I never can carry all the counties in my

head. Happystowe-on-Sea is the name of it;
none of your blessed sewers there. I know a
man who boils there, twice a week; he would
let you in as a visitor, of course, and you would
get the nourishment of his air. Barlow his
name is, Billy Barlow; a rising man in compos,
and cocoa; he has found a way to make one out
of the other, and both of them out of old shoes,
I believe; and I thought of running down to
him, to get a wrinkle; but Mrs. W. seemed to
think there was something *infra dig* in it."

"We cannot be too particular, in my humble
opinion," said Mrs. Windsor, "not only not to
admit any shadow of fraud, into our own transactions, but in no way to countenance any one
tainted with secrets, however lucrative."

"That is the true way of looking at things:
all on the square, ma'am, and all above board.
And nothing else answers in the long run,
does it? However," continued my father, "if
I should by any chance be down that way, I
might like to look in at Barlow's works,—
without letting him know who I was, of course.
I should understand all his devices, at a glance."

"He would know me in a moment, if I went down;" Mr. Windsor was trying not to wink at father; "but he never would guess that you were in the trade, if you wear your blue coat, and brass buttons, the one that makes the boys call you 'the Admiral.' And by the seaside, that would be the proper thing. Only fair play, Bubbly, and honour bright. Snacks—as our Jack says—in whatever you find out."

"Pooh!" cried father; "after all our experience, what could a country bumkin teach us? Ah, Mrs. Windsor, what things we could tell you, if ladies' nerves were stronger! But, John, I've a great mind to take your advice, and encourage the policy of our noble Government, in doing me a good turn, as early as they can. We will get away before those unprincipled Rads can serve their skulking summons. That Joe Cowl means to get up to-morrow, after shamming to be dead for a fortnight,—a Conservative sweep would have cured his cold, by stopping up a chimney—and on Friday he goes for his summons, I hear. The Beak is a Rad, and will let him have it. I shall trust you to keep it all dark about us, and mum's the address of our luggage, and letters. But Friday will find all the Upmore family stowed away happy, at Happystowe."

My father was ever a man of his word. He made his arrangements for half-time boiling, and the completion of all contracts, and left money enough for a fortnight's work, and then we set off in the soap-van; with old *Jerry* in the shafts, and a hamper of good things, and our best clothes on, and *Grip* sitting up in front, and the tilt hanging down, as if by accident, over the third hoop from the back, so that nobody could tell that we had got a bit of luggage. And we jogged along up the Lane first towards Hampstead, so that all the neighbours thought we were going for a pic-nic, as indeed we thoroughly deserved to do, and they wished us a pleasant day and no rain; for they all had a kindly will to us. But as soon as we had thanked them, and got them out of sight, what did father do but turn old *Jerry*, and take the shortest cut to Shoreditch?

At that time, London was not such a thorough

rat-warren of railways as it is now; and although I had travelled by steam before, it was new enough to be delightful. We were going by a line, which was then considered the most dangerous in Great Britain; and this made my mother put her head out of the window, in her anxiety about me, and father, whenever there was anything at all to see. We wanted to look out for ourselves; but she declared that she understood things best; and there was no chance of getting at the other window, because four people put a cloth along their knees, and went on eating, for leagues, and hours. So my father went to sleep, and I tried to get peeps (behind dear mother's bonnet) of the far world flying by. With all my heart I longed to see the sea, of which I had heard so many things, wonderful, terrible, and enchanting. My mother had bought me a straw-hat, with a blue ribbon on it, like a gallant sailor's; and she should have endeavoured, after that, to show me the sea, if it ever came in sight. But nothing that I could say—though I never stopped bothering, as she called it—would keep her attention to that point; and I found out afterwards the reason for it; she was not at all sure about knowing the sea, when she saw it, and was afraid of making some mistake.

"What do I care about the sea?" said father, rather grumpily, when I pestered him. "People call it the sea, because you can't see it. Or if you do, you can't see anything else. I would much rather have a good London fog. Go to sleep, boy; and don't keep jerking at my legs so."

My father had been out of sorts for some time, which had made it desirable that he should come away, even without any summons against him. His appetite was queer, and he wanted setting up. Before Mr. Windsor came urging him so, I heard him say to mother,

"A leg of mutton goes twice with me now; and I call that a very serious sign."

"Then be more free-handed with your money," answered mother.

And now he was touchy, because poor *Grip*, though accustomed to living in a tub at school, was aggrieved at the box which the Company

provided for dogs on their travels, and expressed
his grief in a howl, that out-howled the engine.
His chest was capacious, and his lungs elastic,
his heart also of the finest order; and for these
gifts of nature, my father condemned him!

"Now, rouse up, rouse up, everybody;"
father shouted, as if we had all been asleep—
which he alone had been, in spite of *Grip*—
when the bus from the "Happystowe Road,"
(which was five or six miles from the genuine
Happystowe) pulled up, in a ring of newly
planted trees, and in front of a porch with
square pillars to it. "Tommy, look sharp, and
count all our boxes in. Put them down in
Latin, if it comes more easy. Sophy, accept
my arm, up the steps; never pretend to be
younger than you are. Mrs. Roaker, we are
come to spend a week with you, if agreeable,
and not too expensive."

"Mr. Upmore!" said mother, in a tone of
quiet dignity, such as she had heard Mrs.
Windsor use; "as if a few pounds made any
difference to you! We are out for the holidays,
and we mean to have them."

"Then the thing to begin with is a rattling good dinner," father answered, without any dignity at all; "bless my—something the dinner goes into, Mrs. Roaker,—if it isn't going on for seven o'clock! And nothing all the way, but hard boiled eggs, and a cold duck, and ham sandwiches. I never was so hungry in all my life; starving is the proper word for it. What can we have for dinner, ma'am, and what is the shortest time for it?"

"Anything you please to name, sir;" said the landlady, who understood things; "and the time will naturally depend upon the nature of the *plats* you order."

"No foreign kickshaws, and no French plates, for me, ma'am! A pair of fried soles, and a bit of roast mutton, hot from the fire, and a cold apple-pie. Sophy, can you think of anything else you want?"

"Can we have a bedroom with a fine sea-view?" My mother had been pensive all day, and religious, because of leaving home, and of the dangers of the train. "We have not seen the sea yet, Mrs. Roaker, to our certain knowledge. You must not suppose us to be any sort of Cockneys; and indeed we live quite outside of London, in a beautiful place, with green fields round it; still we are what you may call in-landers, and we feel a kind of interest in the sea."

"Sophy, you had better order dinner, after that;" said my father, very shortly; "now, Tommy, you be off. I am not going out, till I've had my dinner. But I can't stand any more of your plague about the sea. Find somebody to show you where it is; or you ought to find it out, by the row it makes. I hear a noise now, like an engine with the steam slack. But don't tumble into it, when you find it; though you never were born to be drowned, that I'll swear."

Without any answer to this cut at me,—which I did not deserve, as old Rum could have told him—I whistled for *Grip*, who was looking about, after running all the way from the station, for any dog anxious to insult him; and as soon as he came, and made a jump at me, we set off together without more ado, to find out where the sea was, by the noise it made; of which I was beginning now to read in Homer.

CHAPTER IX.

THALATTA!

IT was five years now, since I had first gone up, (without any intention of doing so) from the surface of the earth into the regions of the air, through the sudden expansion of my heart and system, at the thought of three days' holiday. In the interval, there had been times of elation and elevation, when it was difficult for me to keep down, and the mere shake of an elbow would have sent me up. And among them, I recollect one Christmas-eve, when there was a hard frost on, and the people at the Hampstead ponds were skating, and the ice was all green for boys to slide on, and the trees on the hill were all feathered with snow, and Jack Windsor came up to me, and said, "plum-pudding for dinner, at your house, Tommy; I smelled it, as I came up the Lane "—I was all on the flutter to fly, and astonish the people, who were putting skates on; and I could not have helped it—for there was nothing to lay hold of—if *Grip* (who was full of my bodily welfare) had not laid hold of me by the tails of the scarlet comforter, which mother had knotted so tightly, that I could not get it off.

"Get away, you vile dog! Go up, Tommy," Jack Windsor cried, and would gladly have kicked *Grip*, if prudence had permitted it; "oh, Tommy, do go up; I have heard so much about it, and I'd give anything to see you fly!"

For my part, I was not at all afraid; my feet were off the ground, and there is very little doubt, that I should have escaped from the comforter, and *Grip*, if Jack had not made such a stupid fuss about it.

"Halloa there! What are you boys doing?" A heavy policeman came grumbling along, without any sense of the situation; "if you don't move on, and take that beast of a dog further, I'll walk you pretty quick to the station."

"331 V.," answered Jack, who inherited his mother's lofty style, "if you knew who we are, you'd employ your cheek to keep your tongue in, and save me the trouble of reporting you."

The constable pretended not to hear him; but the whole of my volatile power was gone—so sensitive has it always been—and instead of going up to the sky, I was glad to sit down upon the broad back of the faithful dog.

And now, I can assure you, and you will readily believe it, that having been plagued so long by boys, (and grown-up people, quite as troublesome, at times) concerning what had happened to me, at an early age, and being rebuked, and jeered, and scoffed at—sometimes for having this gift, and sometimes for not making more of it, and sometimes for setting up a false claim to it—young as I was, I had thought a good deal, and made up my mind, in fifty different ways, about it.

But though my conclusions perpetually varied, there was one grain of wisdom to be found in all. It had pleased Heaven, to afflict me with an unusually light corporeal part, and then to relieve that affliction, in some measure, by the gift of a buoyant and complacent mind; so that I was

able—unless a bad cold, or measles, or mumps,
or chilblains stopped me—to be hopeful that all
would turn out for the best, and to keep my
nature boyish, throughout a boyhood of some
perplexity.

Grip, though faithful, and sage, as almost all
the patriarchs put together, might still be considered a juvenile dog, by those who dwell chiefly
on the right side of things. To say that his
heart was still in the right place, would be little
less than an insult to him, and to the great race
of which he was one; but it is not so wholly a
matter of course, that his mind was still ardent,
and his spirit lofty. Very few " Scientists " of
any candour could have looked at *Grip*, when
prepared for battle (with his ears pricked up,
and his neck on the rasp, and his tail set with
stiffening bulges) without finding a nobler result
of evolution, and a likelier survival, than their
own.

His thankful spirit had not yet exhausted
the joys of freedom from the Railway box; and
perhaps—though it is not for me to say it—the
Happystowe air was more mercurial than that of

our works, which confined his meditations too
persistently to one theme—bone. But let that
pass; it is quite impossible to explain everything that happens; all I know is that *Grip* set
off from the porch of the *Twentifold Arms Hotel*,
with a flourish, and a scurry, and a gambol of
delight. With a gentle breeze moving behind
me, I started, to catch him and get the first sight
of the sea ; and then, down a steep path, we came
round the corner of what must have been a live
rock, and behold——

Behold! was a word you might have shouted
at me, like thunder, without my knowing it.
Because my whole nature was absorbed in beholding, or gazing, or staring, or mooning, or
being bemooned—for the things were done to
me, without my doing any one of them. Behind
me, shone the low summer sun, throwing out my
shadow any length it pleased, on an endless,
measureless, countless, unimaginable world of
silver, like the moon come down.

If I could have uttered any syllable, to let off,
or thought of any definite idea, to keep in the
wondrous inconceivable expansion of my nature,

perhaps, even now, I might have stayed upon the
ground. But being as I was, away I went,
starting, at a height of about ten feet above the
level of Spring-tides, with a moderate Westerly
breeze behind me, and the light of the sinking
sun coming up, under the soles of my shoes, as
I slowly went round. And unluckily I had all
my best clothes on—new from a shop down in
Liverpool Street, the first Sunday of the summer
holidays.

People, who have never been up like this,
might suppose, at first sight, that I was terrified; especially at being carried out to sea, as
my first acquaintance with that great space.
But without laying claim to any share of courage,
I may state, as a simple matter of fact, that I
happened to feel no fear whatever. My father,
(as truthful a man as ever lived, and from whom
I inherit that quality) had said that I never was
born to be drowned; and if I thought at all
(which I disremember doing) that alone would
have reassured me. At any rate, I looked
around, as calmly as if I were sitting down to
dinner; but with this disadvantage, that I could

not keep my gaze very firmly fixed upon anything, because of the rotation of my body. For
instance, I was able to shout down to *Grip* (who
was howling most mournfully in the gap, and
making sad jumps to come after me) that I
was all right, and would come back, by and by;
but before I could judge whether he was con-
soled, my eyes were on a ship a long way out.
If there had been much wind, perhaps it would
have proved a ticklish thing for me; but the air
was calm, and full of yellow light, the sea was
below me, like a floor of silver, the sky of a pure
soft blue, wherever the sun did not interfere
with it; and nothing on any side suggested
danger, or uneasiness.

But, whatever the state of things may be, the
human element is certain to rush in, and spoil
all the comfort of nature. I had not been at all
disconcerted, at perceiving that some people on
the beach were surprised by my appearance, at
a considerable height above their heads. They
were calling out loudly to one another, and running together, or running away, and rubbing
their eyes, as if the sun had taken the accuracy

out of them. This rather pleased me, and improved my flight (which depends very much upon the approval of mankind), and I was beginning to practise movements, which I had thought of, and heard of from Jack Windsor. Jack had been taking swimming lessons, and being a wonderfully heavy fellow, had tried very hard to keep his head up. He had learned the whole theory of it beautifully, and showed me how easy it was to do; but as yet he had never been able to do it. Whatever I have done above the surface of the earth — which people are stupid enough to call flying—is nothing more than swimming in the air, or floating; or best of all, perhaps, I should say treading, as people who are heavy enough "tread water." And my great desire was to be my own master, to steer myself a little, as a man can do in swimming; instead of going round and round, at the air's discretion, like a bunch of lime-berries in September.

But, just as I was learning with my hands and feet, and some guidance of the silken summer tunic at my hips,—what did I discover but a great

long gun, taken up by a man, from a boat upon
the beach, and then being pointed with a careful
aim at me! I endeavoured to scream out—"I am
Tommy; only Tommy Upmore going for a fly;
if you shoot me, you will be hanged for murder!"
—but I give you my word that my fright was so
great, that no sound of any use would come out
of my mouth. Old Rum's cane was quite a joke,
compared to this. Every atom of my levity
turned to lead, my hands fell to my sides, and
my feet struck together, and I dropped, like a
well-bucket, when the rope is broken.

And I never had a luckier drop in my life—
good as it is for all mortals to come down—for
just above my hair, (which had been floating,
like a sunset cloud, they say, but was now
standing out, like a badger's, with alarm) a
heavy charge of duck-shot, that would have
killed *Grip* dead, went whistling like a goods'-
train engine; and a streak of white still may be
discovered in my head, from the combination of
fear and fact.

And my drop was quite as lucky at the lower
end; for descending, as you might say without

exaggeration, almost vertically, (though my head, the lightest portion of my system, still was up) instead of falling into the sea, I was received in a sail, spread to catch me by a very lovely boat.

Some moments elapsed, as I have reason to believe, before either my rescuers, or myself, were fit to go into all the questions that arose. Naturally enough, they were surprised at the style of my visit to them; while I was not only embarrassed by shyness, at finding myself among great people, but also to some extent confused in mind, from the many gyrations of my upward, and the rapid descent of my downward course; moreover, I had never been in a boat till now, and the motion of the boards upon the water disconcerted me, more than any action of the air.

But while I was balancing myself like this, after stepping from the sail that was spread for me, a beautiful lady, who had been sitting on a fur, and looking at me with surprise and interest, arose and came towards me, with some little doubt enlarging the brightness of her large bright eyes.

"Why, you are a boy—a boy!" she cried, as if Nature ought to have made me a girl; "and as pretty a boy as I ever beheld. From the way you went round, and the height it was up, I thought it must be a machine at least—one of those wonderful things they invent, to do almost anything, nowadays. Whatever you are, you can speak, I am sure; and I am not going to be afraid of you. Where do you come from? And what is your name? And how long have you been up in the air, like that? And have you got any father, and mother? And how did you get such most wonderful hair, like spun silk, every bit of it? And—and, why don't you answer me?"

"If you please, ma'am," I said, looking up at her with wonder, for I never had seen such a beautiful being, although I had been to a play, several times; "I was trying to think, what question you would please to like me to begin with answering. I'm afraid that I cannot remember them all, because of my head going round so. But my name is 'Tommy Upmore,' and I come from Maiden Lane, St. Pancras."

" St. Pancras! Why, that is in London,
surely. Did you come in a balloon, or how can
you have done it? Sit down and rest; I am
sure you must be tired. Though you look like
a rose, Master Tommy Upmore."

I answered the beautiful lady, as soon as
presence of mind permitted, that I had not
come the whole way from London, through the
sky, as she seemed to suppose, but only from
yonder place on the shore; where I showed
her *Grip*, still howling now and then, and
striving with all his eyes, and heart, to make
sure what was become of me. She replied that,
even so, it was in her opinion wonderful; and
she doubted if she could have been brought
to believe it, unless she had seen it with her
own eyes. I told her that several most eminent
men of science saw nothing surprising in it; but
accounted for it easily, in various ways, without
any two having to use the same way.

Meanwhile she was begging me not to be
afraid, herself having now overcome all fear;
and she signed to the boatmen (who had fallen
back, with their frank faces wrinkled, as a

puzzle is) that they might come forward, and be kind to me. It was not in their power to do this, because they had not yet finished staring; therefore she offered me her own white hand, and I wished that I had washed mine lately.

"These are my children," she said, as I followed her down the planks, without a word; "it was Laura, who saw you first up in the air, and Roly who ordered the men to row over, when that wicked young man put his gun up. We thought it was some new kind of bird. And so you are—a boy bird! Roly, and Laura, let me introduce you to this young gentleman. There is nothing about him to be afraid of, although he has come down from the clouds, or rather from the clear sky, this beautiful evening. He declares that he can be scientifically explained; and when that can be done, there is nothing more to say. Roly has never known what fear is, ever since he cut his teeth."

From all I have seen of this gentleman since then—and I have seen a great deal of him for twenty years, and never can see too much of him—I can fully confirm what his dear mother said. Just then, he was a boy of about my age, or a year or two older he might be; but pounds, and tens, and twenty pounds, heavier, and an inch or two taller, and many shades darker. I was as fair in complexion, before a great mob of troubles came darkening me, as if I had sprung from a boiling of Pontic wax, besprinkled with roses of Cashmere. But Roly (or to give him his full deserts, Sir Roland Towers-Twentifold) was a dark, and thoughtful, and determined lad, who meant to make his mark upon our history, and is doing it.

He came up, and took my hand, as if he would squeeze any cloudiness out of me; and nothing but the pinches I had often had at school, enabled me to bear it without a squeak. He had been at the helm, as they call it, to direct the boat the right way to catch me; and although he was greatly surprised, he concluded—as all Englishmen do upon such occasions—that the time to explain things would ensue, after they had been dealt with.

CHAPTER X.

To me, who am accustomed to myself, it has always seemed much more wonderful, that my father should deny my peculiar powers, than that I should possess them. "Go up, Tommy," he has said a thousand times; "don't be so shy about it, but up with you! The proof of the pudding is in the eating. Only fly up to the bedroom window-sill, as that little sparrow from the road has done, and I'll own that I'm a fool, and you a wonder. But, until you have done it, in my sight, my son, I shall stick to my old experience, that all the human race are liars, but not one of them a flyer."

His strong opinion proved-itself, as the manner of strong opinions is; and instead of being able

to arise, while he was waiting, with his hands
in his pockets, and a pipe in his mouth, I was
more inclined to go into the ground, whenever it
happened to be soft.

And so, even now, (when some fifty people
had seen me in the air, and were ready to make
oath to a great deal more than I had done)
father stuck to it, that they all were liars, or
fools, or crazy, or else tipsy at the least. But
he scarcely knew what to say at first, when
just as he was going to sit down to dinner, a
mighty great noise arose under the window, of
sailors hurraing, and the brass-band roaring,
and *Grip* as loud as any of them, barking at
his utmost.

"D—n it," said my father to my mother;
"is this the quiet place John Windsor spoke
of? When a man can't even sit down to his
dinner——"

"Dinner indeed! Don't think twice of your
dinner;" cried mother from the window, in
great excitement, "here is a thing that you
never saw before, and will never see again, if
you live to be a hundred. Our Tommy in a

flag, and all the sailors in the kingdom, taking off their hats, and cheering him, and the dear little poppet as modest as ever, exactly like an Angel! And a beautiful lady, you can see by the look that all the place belongs to her—you can tell at a glance who she is, of course—Bucephalus, how slow you are!"

"Slow, for not knowing at a glance a female, I never saw or heard of, in all my life! And in a strange place I was never in before! How should I know her from Adam—or at least, Eve?"

"Bucephalus! Why, of course she must be Lady Towers-Twentifold, widow of the late, and sincerely lamented, Sir Robert Towers-Twentifold, who died, after tortures surpassing description, from swallowing his own corundum tooth. Every stick, and stone, for ten miles in every direction belongs to him, and he leaves a lovely widow, and an only son, the present Sir Roland Towers-Twentifold, scarcely any older than our Tommy, and an only daughter Laura. Bless me, how true everything is coming! I can believe every word of it, now I see them."

"Including the man with the corundum tooth.

In the name of Moses, Sophy, how the deuce have you found out all this already?"

"I have found out nothing; and I am surprised at your low way of putting it, Bucephalus. When I met the chambermaid, could I do less than pass the time of day to her? But look, they have carried our Tommy three times, with the 'Conquering Hero comes' twice and a half, round the—I forget what dear Jane Windsor says is the right foreign name for it—and I think, Mr. Upmore, the least we can do, is to throw up the window, and bow our acknowledgments gracefully, as the papers say."

"I'm blowed if I'll do anything of the sort. Half a crown's worth of coppers would be gone in no time. Keep behind the curtain, Sophy; or back we all go to business to-morrow morning; and I heartily wish we had never come away. At home, when I am hungry, I can get my dinner."

"Oh dear, he has spoiled his white ducks with tar, and *Grip* is in a dreadful mess of wet, and the sailors want to hoist him too, if he would only let them! I see what it is—how stupid of

me! Tommy has been flying all over the sea,
and *Grip* has been swimming after him! Oh,
Bucephalus, how can you eat your dinner? Is
this a proper time, for you to be devouring
dinner?

"You are right enough there, Sophy;"
answered father, "I ought to have had it five
hours ago. I call it tempting Providence with
one's constitution, to go so long after breakfast-
time. I only hope, the zanies won't come wanting to hoist me."

Alas, that the stronger of my parents should
have shown such incredulity! Did it follow that,
inasmuch as he was heavy, all his productions
must draw the beam? If so, dead must drop
all the wit of Falstaff, and all the sweet humour
of Thackeray. And how could my father have
made light sperm, or the soap, that he labelled
"the froth of the sea"? Such questions, however, come dangerously near to science, and its
vast analogies. Enough, that my father paid
dear in the end, for all this incredulity; as will
be made manifest, further on; and sorry shall
I be to tell it.

My dear mother was already of opinion, that it was a crime upon any one's part, even to attempt to explain my achievements, and down-right treason to deny them. When the beautiful Lady Twentifold—as people called her for convenience, though her proper name was *Towers-Twentifold*—came, when the public was tired of shouting, to learn all that could with propriety be learned, of the origin of her " great little wonder," few people verily would believe what my mother was fanciful enough to do. The lady (to whom the hotel belonged, and all the people there, in my opinion) sat down in the parlour downstairs, with my hand in hers—for she had taken dear liking to me, because I resembled a child she had lost—and she begged the land-lady to go to my mother, without any card or formality, and ask whether she might have the pleasure of seeing, and telling her about her boy.

It is a very clumsy thing for me to find fault with the behaviour of my parents, and I am not prepared to do so now. There may have been fifty reasons, clear to people much wiser than myself; but certainly I was amazed, and angry, when Mrs. Roaker came back to say, that the lady from London was so fatigued, with the dreadful effects of her journey, that she begged to thank her ladyship most warmly, for very great kindness to her dear son; but felt quite unequal to an interview with her.

"How many of you are there, Tommy?" Lady Twentifold asked, without my knowing why. But she always went straight to the meaning of things.

"Only me, ma'am, if you please;" I answered, looking up, in fear that there ought to have been more; "but I did hear a woman say, that there had been another; but he went to heaven, before me, I believe."

The lady looked at me, with her eyes quite soft, which they had not been, when she received that message; and she seemed to be uncertain, whether she was right, in putting her next question.

"Has your father been married more than once, my dear? I mean, is this lady your own dear mother, or become your mamma, since you can remember?"

I told her, that I could not remember any one thing about it, though I often thought. But this was my mother, Mrs. Upmore; everybody said so; and more than that, there was nobody else in all the world, who made a quarter so much of me.

"Tommy, I am quite satisfied upon that point," she answered; "there may be some reason, which I do not know of. Or perhaps your dear mother is not at all strong. Give her my compliments, and say that I hope she will be better soon, and the Happystowe air relieve her weakness. Now shake hands with Roly, and little Laura; and good-bye till we see you again, flying Tommy."

I had told her that my name was "flying Tommy;" and she was much pleased to hear it, because it showed, that the Happystowe air was not to blame, for my adventure. Then Sir Roland came up, and took my hand, and said that he hoped I would take him for a fly; and then, the most beautiful child, I had ever set eyes on, stole up shyly, and put her little hand in mine, and left me to say good-bye to her.

On the following day, I felt as heavy as *Grip* (who weighed half a pound for every ounce that a human being of his size would weigh), and my father and my mother agreed, from different points of view, about me,—that I must be kept indoors, and fed, and put at my books, to steady me. We had brought some Greek in the bottom of a box, which father considered great nonsense, though it might be very good for children. And he told me to find out the Greek for soap, and spermaceti, and steam-engine, and write them down, so that he could read them; which I entirely failed to do. Meanwhile he set off, with his Admiral's coat, to inspect the sea and the shipping, and Mr. Barlow's boiling premises.

The day after that again was Sunday, when the rule of our house, and of most houses in Maiden Lane, was to lie in bed until nine o'clock, and have breakfast at ten, and attend to the dinner till dinner-time, and saunter in the fields towards Highgate, if the weather was fine in the afternoon, and to go to church, or chapel, some-times, if there was nothing else to do in the

evening; and then have a good supper, and be
off to bed. But now mother said, and my father
was quite unable to gainsay it, that, being in a
country place like this, where everything depends
upon example, with my father acknowledged to
be an Admiral—not only because of his coat,
and occasional d—ns, and general demeanour,
but also because he had shaken his head, when
requested to look at a ship through a spy-glass
for twopence, and told the ancient tar that he
had seen a deal too much of that—moreover
with Tommy adored by all the aristocracy of the
neighbourhood, and by the brave sailors, and
people of less refinement, accepted as an angel,
the least we could do was to make an effort, and
try to be at church by eleven o'clock.

My father replied, that as concerned himself
there need be no difficulty whatever, because as
soon as he had done his breakfast, his only
preparation was to smoke a pipe; but he did not
believe that it was possible for mother, (who had
spent all Saturday in the village-shops, because
she had come in such hurry from home, that she
had brought nothing fit to be seen in) to have all

her toggery spick-and-span, and her hair done
up to the nines, so early. But, if only to show
him how little he knew, my mother was ready
before he was; and father declared that she
ruined his sleep, having got up to see the sun
rise upon the sea, and stopped up to see herself
grow brighter, and brighter, in the looking-glass.
Dear mother had a great mind not to go to
church, with such a wicked story ringing in
her ears; until father told her that she looked
stunning, and was fit to be put on a transparent lid—the lid of a box of transparent
soap.

"Dear Bucephalus, now you see," she said,
as she placed her primrose glove, on the sleeve
of his blue coat with brass buttons, "one little
portion perhaps of the reason, which led me to
decline an interview, that night, with Lady
Towers-Twentifold. My main reason was, of
course, that I knew so thoroughly well what
ladies are. If I had allowed her to see me, and
satisfy all her great curiosity, about this wonderful darling of a Tommy, the chances are ten
to one, that her ladyship would never have

invited him to Twentifold Towers. But now, I
intend that he shall go there; and what will
the Windsors say to that?"

"Well, that was a very fine reason, Sophy.
But I don't see the other, that I ought to
see."

"Then Tommy is sharper than you, ten times.
But walk a little better, if you please, my dear.
Who can take you for an Admiral, if you drag
your feet like that?"

From a joke, Mr. Windsor's idea had grown
into a great and solid fact. Mrs. Roaker, and
most of the Happystowe people, had made up
their minds by this time, that my father was
"Admiral Upmore." He was too honest, and
plain a man, to encourage this mistake for a
moment, and, whenever he got the chance,
declared most stoutly, that he was no Admiral.
The public, however, would not believe him,
having met with some indications in commercial dealings with him, that he prized the
royal effigy; from which it was clear, what his
motive was in desiring to disguise his rank.
And the Boots of the *Twentifold Arms* could

swear that he saw *Admiral* printed, on the back of the label of a hairy trunk, which had only B. U. on the front of it. And so he did, to a certain extent; for mother had taken an advertising card beginning with *Admirable*, and cut it across, and put father's initials on the other side.

"They may call me what they like," my father said, when tired of contradiction, " so long as they don't charge me for it. *Admiral* Upmore serves my turn, uncommonly well, for two things. Billy Barlow would lock his gate, if he knew that I am only Boiler Upmore ; and I am finding out some fine things there. And again, if any lawyer comes sneaking after my heels, with that chummy's process, he'll find his mistake in the visitor's list. But, Tommy, you'll catch it, if you let out a word of this in Maiden Lane. Why, I never should hear the last of it ! "

And so the whole three of us went to church ; and the sailors sitting on the tombstones—most of which were like chests of drawers, but without any handles to the names below—touched their hats to the Admiral's lady, and the gallant

Admiral himself, and the smart little chap, who
had been for a fly, like the cherub aloft, who
smiles luck to poor Jack. It was one of dear
mother's proudest moments—for the men at our
works would never touch their hats, unless they
had been tipped a shilling quite lately—and
she bowed with her feathers (which had been a
cock's) throwing off quite a flash, and a rustle;
until she was compelled to look very grave, by
the remark of an ancient tar, that he had never
seen so fine a woman.

But alas, how fate does ring her changes
with articulate-speaking mortals—the triumph
of the chime, the hesitation of the back-stroke,
and the toll of disappointment! Ere ever
the bells in the tower had ceased, and the
organ taken up the tale, dear mother was a
pensive-hearted female, and her feathers out of
plume. For in coming up the aisle, she had
whispered to the buxom pew-opener; "Lady
Towers-Twentifold has been seeking to make my
acquaintance. Can we sit anywhere near her
pew?"

"Certainly, ma'am;" said Mrs. Button,

turning the handle of a large enclosure; "the Admiral, and yourself, can have her ladyship's pew, this morning, and this evening too, if you come again. Her ladyship has fifteen pews, in the fifteen parishes she owns, and she takes them all in turn; and it won't be our turn, for ten Sundays yet."

CHAPTER XI.

LARGE IDEAS.

PERHAPS it was lucky for me, that my mother had failed to amaze Lady Twentifold, with the elegance of her apparel. But after having taken all that trouble, and lost all her comfort of the morning, she felt it no less than a personal slight, that her ladyship should have disgraced herself so, by neglecting divine worship.

"But she went to some other church," said father.

"I don't believe a word of it," answered mother, with both hands on her prayer-book; "she spent her whole morning in bed, no doubt. I never could endure those slothful ways; and the less we have to do with such people, the better."

" Why, who ever dreamed of our having anything to do with them ? " My father was astonished at any new idea always. " Sophy, I won't have this rubbish any more. I came down here, to enjoy myself, and live well, and improve my liver; as well as to bilk the vile harpies of the law, and find out Billy Barlow's tricks. But if I'm to put out my pipe, and smoke wet rolls (like Tom's taffy-sucks), and never be seen in my shirt-sleeves, and never get a smell of hot meat, till the bats are about, and be cut short of my d—ns indoors, and backed up in them out of doors,—why the world will have come to such a stuck-up pitch, as would soon turn me into a Radical."

My mother said less, but pondered more. In by-gone days, she had seemed content with the place in which she found herself, proud of the works, and the sample-boxes, and our renown for quality; and insisting upon it, that we should be styled in all transactions " Upmore & Co." But lately, or indeed for a long time now, her mind had been taking an elevated tone, which lowered the quality of our victuals. She talked

a great deal more of honour, and much less
of honesty; she began to look down upon the
Sunday papers; and she would not let her
friends say "Ma'am" to her. My father declared, that this disease began with my going
to the *Parthencion*, and was made much worse
by Mrs. Windsor, and the four professors, and
was now turned into a pestilence, by these
bathing-machines, and the sailors at the church,
and the brass-horn rogues coming round with
the cap, and "my lady, if you please," upon the
sands.

This "growth of refinement" as dear mother
called it,—"spread of humbug" was my father's
name for it—turned her attention, quite suddenly, to what she called my associations. The
habit of my body, and mind, had been that of
London boyhood in general,—to rush into anything going on, without waiting for an introduction, to give my opinion without invitation
upon any public spectacle, or even a proceeding
intended to be private until I came round the
corner, and upon every occasion to ignore
humanity's false exclusiveness. But on Monday

morning, when we sat down to look at the
people bathing—which my father, from some
old-fashioned feeling, would never stop to do,
but kept his distance,—mother began to give
me a lesson, concerning the duties of society.

"Tommy," she said, "did you remark that
the little boys go into one machine, and the
little girls into the other? And they are not
allowed, by the Board of Health, to be less than
fifty yards apart."

"Yes, mother," I replied, "I was looking at
that ; and it seems to be the order on the board.
But somehow they seem to contrive, in spite of
it, to get all together in the water. And the
girls—if I can make out which they are—seem
to go all the way over to the boys ! The board
says that they will be prosecuted, with the extreme rigour of the law. There goes another
girl, I declare ! "

"Hush, Tommy, hush ! Or society will expel
us, like a pair of Parians. What I want you
to notice, for your own good, is that high society
has rules quite different from what the children
in the street have. You, unluckily, have been

permitted, while your father was in a smaller
way of business, to associate with almost any
boy of respectable trousers, in the roadway. I
admit that I have not been as strict as I should
be, partly because it was no good. But now
it is high time to draw the line. You see how
they put a cord along down there? Now what
do you suppose they do it for?"

"I am sure I don't know, mother; unless it
is, for people to tumble over it."

"No, Tommy, no. It is to keep the people
out. The inferior classes must not come inter-
fering with those who can pay for all the room
they want. Your father is a Tory; but I begin
to think, that I shall be a Radical; because I
find them make people pay more, for getting
into anything. A ticket for a week, for both of
us, to see the people bathe, and dress their hair,
and everything, was only half a crown for me,
and fifteenpence for you, my dear! And you
may sit, all the time, on the ground of the earth,
which is so much cleaner than the seats they
make. Come into this hole, with the rushes on
the top—where I dare say some wild animal has

lived—and never mind the people in the waves, my dear. What I want you to be, is a great man, Tommy; a very great man, who may look down upon the little ones, and remember (when he has lost his own dear mother) that he owes all his greatness to her counsel, and high principles."

My dear mother spoke with such depth of feeling—especially in reference to her own end —that I had not the least idea what to say, and did not like to cry, until I had waited for some more.

" School-life is hardening you, my son ; " she said. " I have known the day, when you would have been crying long ago, at the description of all that I go through. However, it is all for the best, and my own doing. I must expect you to grow up. And grown-up men must never cry. Tommy, you can have two bull's-eyes, out of my pocket, if you know where to find them, while I am wiping my poor eyes. They were under my handkerchief right side down, and the old pair of gloves on the top of them, that I put on when the promenade is over. You have got them, my son? Well, take one at a time, and don't bite them, until I have said a few words. Don't be afraid, Tommy. I am not going to deliver a lecture, such as nobody ever that knows me could expect of me. You will have a great mind, my dear, as well as five talents of the body that will come to five and twenty, when the woman begins to sweep the house. And with all these great blessings of the Lord upon you, your first duty is to keep them all to yourself. That was one reason, why I would not come out, when they made such a fuss about you, the other night. They had no right to come between you and me; and heartily thankful as I felt to them, is it likely that I would put up with that sort of thing?"

"But, mother," I could not help saying, "suppose there had been nobody there, when I came down? You were out of sight altogether; and though I might not have gone down through the water, if my legs had gone in, they would have stuck there."

"Don't talk of such dreadful things, my dear. I am speaking sincerely out of gratitude. No one has ever accused your poor mother of any deficiency in that. But I think, that the least Lady Twentifold could do, was to come to church on Sunday, if only to thank the Lord for the service she had been enabled to render you. Few ladies have had such a chance afforded them; but she thinks much more of her fifteen pews. Now, Tommy, if you meet her on the beach, or any of the members of her family, you are not to rush up to them, as if you were under a great obligation, and make them talk large. You may show yourself; but wait for them to accost you, as Mrs. Windsor says. You know what to accost a person means."

"Yes, mother, from *costa*, the Latin for a rib. And it often comes in Homer. 'And thus accosting him in reply spake sovereign Agamemnon.' Old Rum does it like that, nearly always."

"Tommy, what a clever boy you are! I love to hear a bit of Latin from you. But whatever you say to the Twentifold people, you never must speak of your master as 'Old Rum.' It sounds quite low, and it contains no learning. You may speak of Dr. Rumbelow, if you like, and your place of education, the *Pantheon*— though why it should have the same name as a bazaar, I am very much afraid I shall never understand. But mind, more than anything else, my son, what I am going to tell you now. You say that none of them asked you, on Friday, what was your father's path in life."

"No, mother; none of them said a word about it. All they wanted to know was about myself. But I'm not sure, I did not tell about Old Rum."

"Well, it won't matter much, if you did, my dear. But the boys at school call you 'soap,' and 'tallow,' and 'bubbles,' and 'dips,' and a quantity of things; all of which prove how low they are themselves. Now, we will not allow these great people to do that. And the only way to stop them, is not to let them know private matters, that can be no concern of theirs. Above all things, be truthful as the day, my son. Your father is not an Admiral; and you must acknowledge that he is not—supposing

that the question should come up—and if they
want to know any more about him, which
people of any good manners would not, just
tell them (in so many words) the truth—that
your father is a gentleman, the head of his own
firm of merchants in the Metropolis, and invited
to dine at the Mansion-house, from his eminence
in politics."

"But suppose they should ask about the
boiling, mother; and the things that we sell,
and the smell in the Lane—— "

"What a stupe you are! As if you didn't
know by this time, after all the schooling you
have had, that in good society nobody knows
of anything that doesn't smell nice. The
highest of them do all that themselves; but
as for talking of it, and in the presence of
ladies—why it makes them faint. Your mother
is of a good family, Tommy; and you get
your distinguished appearance from her. And
though I did marry a Lightbody first, and after
his time an Upmore, I have often been told
that my ancestors had a knighthood in their
family, which makes it improper for a son

of mine, to say anything about soap-boiling. Moreover, I will tell you, as a very great secret, which you must not say a word about in Maiden Lane, what your father was saying in his sleep, the other night. It was the first night we came down here, and the strange bed, and the kicking noise the sea makes, and the late dinner, and the Welsh rabbit to top up with, perhaps interfered with his natural rest; for he has not told a word of his dreams for years. He thought he was talking to you, my dear, and you were at the top of a ladder, or a tree, so far as I could make out his words. 'Tommy, come down,' he said; 'come down, Tommy; and I'll show you where all the money is put, for you to go into Parliament.' And then I suppose that you wouldn't come down, for he slapped at his leg, where he keeps his money; and he called out louder—'They meddle with me! I'll meddle with them, when it comes to a plum; and let them know who Upmore is. And if I am too old, my son shall do it.' And then he got sore, where he knocked himself; for his hand is heavy, and his veins are large; and

he awoke very grumpy, and rubbed his leg; and
I could not get any more out of him."

"Why, Bill Chumps is going into Parliament!" I cried, being struck by this strange
coincidence; "and I should like to go very
much, wherever he is; and Roly Twentifold is
sure to go too; and we ought to do something
between us, mother, for the good of the country,
and all the poor people, and to make things
fetch more money. I was reading about a great
man, the other day—— "

"I don't want to hear about any great men,
until you are one of them, Tommy. Go and
play on the sands, while I rest for an hour;
this air does make me yawn so. Are you sure
you have got your dumb-bells in your pockets,
and your fisherman's lead round the top of
your stomach? Then whistle for *Grip*, for
there might be Professors down here, for aught
we know of. And come back, as soon as the
London papers are down, if there is anything
about any of us."

In spite of the weight I had now to carry,
for fear of going out to sea again, I ran away

joyfully down the sands, as they call the gravel where the sand should be. At the ring of the steel-whistle which I carried round my neck, *Grip* came bounding from the Inn to meet me, and with mutual confidence we began to poke about, for something to afford a hunt. Then I heard a voice holloaing out, "Hi, Tommy!" and with a long stride, quite like that of a man, Sir Roland Twentifold came down to me.

"Why, I thought you had given us the slip," he shouted, for he always spoke as if he wanted every one to hear; "I came down with my pony on Saturday, but I could not see a sign of you. And I did not like to call at the Inn, because of your mother's bad health, you know. And on Sundays, my mother won't let me go far; because she is religious, and so am I. There are so few fellows who care for that now, that I stick up for it, and mean to do so. I won't have everything turned upside down."

"Take care that my *Grip* doesn't roll you over," I exclaimed, for the dog had no muzzle on; "I can't always hold him, when he takes a dislike."

" *Grip*, come here," he said, "and talk to me. I have got a dozen dogs, who could eat you, *Grip*. But if you are good, they shall be good to you."

I could not help laughing at this idea, for *Grip* could thrash any three dogs I knew. But to my astonishment, *Grip* came up, and wagged his tail softly to Sir Roland, and sniffed about him pleasantly, and then offered his grisly ears for a loving rub.

"Don't be nervous, doggy," went on Sir Roland, as if he were talking to an Italian greyhound; "you smell rather doggy; but I don't mind that. If your master goes for a fly every day, and you swim after him, you'll soon be cured."

"Only fancy," I said, as I pulled his tail, that he might not take up with a stranger so; "he had never seen the sea before, any more than I had; but the moment he knew I was in your boat, in he dashed, to come and look after me. And he is not at all a water-dog, as you must know, having such a lot of dogs of your own. He swallowed such a lot of salt water, that he

could only gurgle, instead of growling, when
the sailors petted him; and I do believe if you
had not managed to get hold of his collar, with
that long stick, he would have been a drowned
dog, the same as I have seen twenty of together,
when the wind blows down the reservoir of the
Water-company. Oh, how sad it must be, for
their Master and Mistress. If *Grip* was to die,
I never should get over it."

"What a soft you are! Why, you are crying
now, with *Grip* all alive to lick your face! Such
a chap, as you, would never do at Harrow. We
should call you 'Fanny,' instead of Tommy
Upmore. Now, don't be offended. You can't
expect to be anything but a muff, after going to
a private school, you know."

"Bill Chumps is not a muff, and he was there
six years. If Bill Chumps heard you talk like
that, he'd take you by the back of the neck, and
throw you over the top of that bathing-waggon."

"I beg your pardon, Tommy," said Sir
Roland, whose nature was truly generous; "it
was cowardly of me to talk like that, when you
can't help yourself, of course. Every fellow

should stick up for his own hole. But what
Bill Chumps are you talking about? There can't
be very many Bill Chumpses, I should think."

"I should rather think not. There is nobody
like him. He is gone to Pope's Eye College
now, at Oxford, with a scholarship founded by
his own father, for the benefit of all descendants.
And they say he gets on wonderfully, though
everybody cut him, for a week or so."

"Well, what a wonderful thing!" cried Roly,
as he told me immediately that I must call
him, unless I wanted to get a flyer; "I was at
Oxford, last Commemoration-time, to see my
cousin, who went up from Harrow, just at the
time when Chumps went up. He is two years
older than I am, and a decent kind of fellow in
his way, but sadly short of what we call *go;*
though he belongs to a bigger lot than I do.
The Earl of Counterpagne is his name, as the
song says about somebody. And your Chumps,
everybody calls him Bill Chumps, had pulled
him out of Sandford Lasher, at the very last
moment to save him from croaking. There
were other men there, who were ready to go in;

but Chumps was first, and though he was not a great swimmer, in he jumped, and pulled him up, when he was all but done for. Bad luck for me, as some people would say; but splendid luck, as I think; for I don't want to go into the House of Lords; and what's the good of your own way, unless you make it?"

"That was just like Bill," I said; "he never stopped to think, unless there was lots of time for it. He means to be a great man, and he will be too."

"That's the sort of fellow, I should like to be. I have often thought of running away from home, and the land, and the money, and all that stuff, and setting up properly on my own account, with two night-gowns, and six day-shirts. Who can give any cuds to a fellow, who starts with a heap of money round his neck? If it were not for my mother, and little Laura, I would have started long ago. Whatever I do, I shall get no credit, because of what those dirty Radicals call my 'enormous social advantages.' By the bye, I do hope you're not a Radical, Tommy."

"I should rather hope not," I said, with grand contempt. "My father is a Conservative; and so am I. Though I don't pretend yet to know so very much about it."

"All the better for that. I will teach you," cried Sir Roland. "I know all about it, ever since I can remember. And when my cousin went to call upon Bill Chumps, as he was bound to do after that, the first thing he saw was a great card stuck in the corner of the glass above his chimney-piece, with a baron of beef, and a haunch of mutton, trimmed with ribbons at the top, and then 'W. Chumps, butcher,' in big letters, and a great lot more about meat below, ending with 'House-lamb, when in season.' My cousin was surprised, but of course he said nothing about it, until he knew Chumps well. And then he asked him why; and Chumps said —'just to see whether you were a snob, or not.' And now I tell you, Tommy, that my cousin just opens his door, and shows out any swell, who pretends to patronise his friend, Bill Chumps. But Chumps keeps his distance, and does not want them."

"Well, I wonder I never heard anything about it. If butcher Chumps had heard of it, wouldn't he talk?"

"I don't suppose Chumps ever said a word about it. He is just that sort of fellow, as they say. They wanted to get him a medal; but he would not hear of it, at any price. I shall make his acquaintance, when I go up; and I intend to get him into Parliament. And you too, Tommy, as soon as you are old enough. Only you must try to grow a bit. You are to come, and stop at our place, when the Admiral goes back to London."

CHAPTER XII.

ALTHOUGH I had seen the Tower of London,—
when our van went to a wharf close by,—and
even the new City prison, and several magnificent
houses built by brewers, all these were nothing
but dirt in my eyes, when they lit upon "Twentifold Towers." This grand building was too long
for a far-sighted man to see it all at once, and
too high for me to think of flying over it, and
the depth that it went to, below the ground, was
enough to make one giddy. And the number of
servants, and the way they did things, and the
little they thought about money, was amazing.

But in spite of all this, I was sad in my heart to
stop behind, even in so grand a place, when my
father and mother were gone back home. For I

thought of all the corners that I knew so well, and
the places in the cinders, where the wind blew
warm, and the holes where you might roast a
big potato, (if you watched the proper time for
clinkering,) and the grassy remainders of great
green fields, where the lark, after warbling in
the sky so long, shut both his wings, and shot
down in silence, to run about, and feel the land,
where he felt that he had been an egg. And
then I thought of several fellows, by no means
grand in trousers, or in manners—such as Joe
Grimes, the blacksmith's boy, and Charley
Turps, son of the carpenter—who could enter into
my views, and let me into theirs, without a bit
of language wasted, and who had forgiven me
by this time, for being what they called a " Latin
Tea-kettle ; " and of whom, by this time, there
could not be one, without a long tale of his own
to unfold, and a long one of mine to feel for.
Moreover, I am not ashamed to own—for the
true shame ought to be upon the other side—
that fat Polly Windsor had promised now, for
more than five years, to be my bride ; and I
wanted to amaze her with a true account of the

things I saw the girls do down here. And as I thought of all these delights, I did not care two pence to be a great man, if my greatness would rob me of half of them.

But before going further, I am bound to stop, and do justice to a man, who was not so very great—any more than I shall ever be—but that which is tenfold rarer now, a truthful, honest, and courageous man.

It was not the loss of two Sunday hats, which changed my father's politics, but the running away of the man who stole them, without leaving his name in the lining. My father began to look beneath the surface, having taken all he heard on trust, till now; and as soon as he hit upon facts, he found that he must not find fault with this man, for running. For now, he was enabled to perceive that the essence of the Liberal is—to run. To run with the current of opinion first, judging from the froth which way it goes; and to run away from his own principles next, because they are bad, while his conscience still is good; to run, with all speed, from the voice of reason; and above all to put his best

foot foremost, in running for his pocket from the
enemies of England.

Having set his mind, and heart, against that
style of going, my father discovered that his own
life grew more honest, and open, in little dealings, from a firmer standard in larger ones.
And though he was here, to some extent,
with a view to smooth the way for a Government contract, and test the true value of Billy
Barlow's tricks; the sterling weight of his principles never fell into the scale of his interests.

"How Tommy may turn out, is more than
I can say," he exclaimed, after reading Lady
Twentifold's letter, in which she apologised
most gracefully, for the liberty she had been
tempted to take, in begging them to spare their
dear bright boy, for a few days' visit at the
Towers, though she had been prevented by
absence from calling upon Admiral, and Mrs.
Upmore; but her dear son, Roland, who would
bring this note, would explain that she had only
just been told of their sudden return to London,
etc., etc., all most pleasing, and put in the
kindest and prettiest way—"whether Tommy

will stick to the business," said father, "and make it pay better than his poor governor—as he calls me, when my back is turned—and be able, by the time he is fifty years old, to pay his way into Parliament, and represent the boiling interest, which is abominably treated there—it lies in the doom of the future to bring forth. But after all the years, I have lived in the world, although I have only been on committees, and never more than vice-chairman, I know too well what Statesmen are. If they can fish up, against one another, so much as the passing of a bad penny-piece, when they were at school together, the man at the top of the tree will never hear the last of it. If our Tommy goes on, as his schooling shows, he may happen to be heard of by and by, though there's nothing wonderful about him yet, except these lies about his flying; and none of the Rads, if he turns out a Tory, and none of the Tories, if he turns into a Rad, shall ever be able to say of him then, that he started under false colours. Hand me one of my invoice-slips; there are three, or four, over in that pocket-book. I'll be as straight-forward as

Bill Chumps was, with the Earl, according to Tommy's tale."

"Oh, what are you going to do?" cried mother; "after all the lecture I gave Tommy, and all I have done on the sands, oh dear! It is flying in the face of Providence."

"The Lord—if you mean Him by 'Providence'—loves the men He has made, to tell the truth; and the women likewise, to the extent of their powers, though not so much insisted on. Sir Roland is gone to the beach with his pony, to wait for your answer, I believe. Tommy shall take it down to him. Read it as you go, my son, and then put it in this envelope."

What I had to read, and deliver, to my affable, yet rather arrogant friend, ran as nearly as may be to this effect:

"Bucephalus Upmore, Son and Successor to the late S. Upmore, of the old-established Boiling and Refining Works, etc., etc.," in large type; and then in good round hand this—"presents his respects to Lady Towers-Twentifold, and begs to thank her, on behalf of self and wife, for your kind invitation to our son,

Thomas. The same is a good boy, and well brought up, so far as can be seen to; and his schoolmaster ready to answer for him, and will never do any disgrace to the business, unless he gets into bad company. But from experience of the world, B. U. expects to hear no more from your ladyship, as soon as she knows all about our Tommy. He can't fly, no more than his father can, and he goes from Happystowe by Railway-bus, as soon as all of us has had our dinner, which was a great mistake in coming down, to start with breakfast only. Offering your ladyship all good wishes, from a happy stay here at Happystowe, remain your obedient servant to command, Bucephalus Upmore, of address above."

Now, it went very much against my grain, to deliver this letter to my friend Roly—for my friend I may call him, by this time, after the things we had done, and enjoyed, together. For I had taught him several ingenuities, such as a London boy can show, of clogging the wheels of the bathing-waggons, and pouring a little tar into the shoes left on the beach by paddlers, and other devices even better; so that we had made rare larks together, and he would find it dull without me.

"All up now," I cried, as he came, at full gallop, for his answer; "the governor has done for all my chance of ever going up to your place. Look what he says! And not half of it is true. We are boilers; but we don't make dips like that."

Sir Roland was looking at a bunch of rush-lights, very well done, but much older than I was—for night-lights had long superseded them —and he could not help laughing, though he tried severely. And I had talked rather largely about commerce, once or twice, when we got into abstract subjects, as we used, when the last chance of a lark was gone. "He has done it on purpose," I said, "to pull me down. Why, he might have used his new bill-heading, quite like a picture you can look at, with a palm in the middle, and an olive full of oil, and two great cannons made into candlesticks, for his Virgin-honey patent that burns like bees, and land-steam on one side, and sea-steam on the other, to show the extent of his transactions. Tell my dear lady, that wretched old thing came down, I am sure, from my grandfather. Oh, what was mother about, to let him ?"

"Admirals are wilful men," replied Sir Roland, seriously regarding that vile bill-head; "and they won't always listen to their wives."

"Did I ever call him an Admiral? Did he ever say he was an Admiral? Did any of us ever tell a single lie, about it?"

"Tommy, my boy, don't be excited," Sir Roland said, as gravely as he could contrive; "I have seen a great deal of the world, though I am young; and of course I was aware, from the very first moment, that you belonged to the commercial classes; which (as I read the other day) are rapidly becoming the mainstay of England, against the wild inrush of anarchy. You know, I told you that, the other night, after we had cut the mooring-ropes of the three machines of the Radical. Very well, if you are in trade, where is the difference between big and little? The retail dealers are the loftier class, because they make less profit. I have thought about these things, for several hours, and I am not misled by what I read. And the conclusion I have come to is just this—that the retail man is of a higher class, in every way, than the wholesale one."

"But," I said, as firmly as I could say it, and proudly repressing all tendency to tears, "we are wholesale, wholesale all over. Even father can't say less than that, when he wants to run down all of us, to keep our ideas from spending."

"Never mind, Tommy, what you are," Sir Roland replied, as he buttoned up his coat; "you may be a gentleman, in any calling, if you don't run other people down. That is the surest sign of a cad; and I've never seen any sign of that, in you. Now, I must be off, like the wind, for home; because I am resolved to come back in time for you. We shall want you, all the more for this, friend Tommy."

"I won't come now, if you ask me;" I called out, as he stuck his legs round his pony; "because I shall know, you are thinking about the dips."

"Keep out your things from the rest, and

have them ready. The Station-bus goes at two o'clock. I shall come with a light trap, at half-past one; and nobody will ask you about coming."

By this he meant, that I should have to come *nolens volens*, as we said at school; but, having more faith in my father's knowledge of the world, I did not expect it. However, with mother's consent, my clothes and books were packed in my own little box, while father laughed, and said, " Please yourselves; so long as they go safe to Maiden Lane." But soon he was obliged to confess his mistake, and let mother triumph over him. For while the bus was standing at the door, and our luggage was going down heavily, and my father, in the window, was taking his last look at a great ship in the dis-tance, a quick light sound of wheels came up the staircase; and running out that way, I saw a horse with his forehead pulled up right against the forehead of the bus-horse, as if they were playing at "conquerors." The new horse was beautiful, and full of pride; and the bus-horse looked at him, with mild reproach, be-

tween his shabby blinkers, as if he were saying
—"Wait till you grow old, and you won't come
flustering a poor horse-brother, with your dash,
and frippery, and self-conceit."

"This for you, ma'am!" cried the Boots to
my mother, running up as if he had no breath
left, from the labour and peril of our boxes,
"and young Master Roland, ma'am,—please,
ma'am, his compliments, and he is waiting for
Master Tommy, ma'am."

"Most polite, and most kind of her ladyship
indeed! Bucephalus, what do you say to that?
Which of us understands good society best; if
you please, my dear, if you please to answer
me? What did I tell you, on Monday week,
Tommy, about what had been in my family?
It requires that kind of preparation, to understand these things, my dear. But he can't go,
with less than a guinea in his pocket. Pull out,
Mr. Upmore."

My father was obliged to do all that, except
that he took five per cent., as the style of the
age is, from the beauty of the guinea; and dear
mother, (bearing a tear of pride in one eye, and

a bigger one of sorrow in the other) went to the bag that her purse was locked in, and got out half a sovereign, and looked at it.

"Don't change it, Tommy," she said, "until you don't know at all how to help it. You are going to be with great people, my pet, and you will have to do things handsomely. But they won't expect a little boy, like you, to stand treat, or tip the maids, or anything of that sort; and if you bring this back to me, you shall have it all to go to school with."

Thus, with more money than I ever had before, or ever could have dreamed of owning, I sat by the side of Sir Roland Towers-Twentifold, and watched him drive his horse, which he did, as he did everything, with the greatest vigour, and capacity. We seemed to go as fast as I could fly—with science, and a strong breeze after me—and *Grip* had to use all his legs to keep up; and I looked back sadly at the poor old bus, with father, and his German pipe, upon the box, and mother with her handkerchief waving from the window; and Roly would not stop, for me to say another word to them.

Now, I need not have told all this, except for the mean charge brought against me, that I got into Twentifold Towers, and thence into public life, by trickery, by false pretences, and imposture on the part of all of us, having conspired among strangers to present my father as an Admiral — " The Admiral of the Fleet-ditch " those unprincipled jokers have dared to call him, because the old Fleet-stream comes down our valley. Possibly, if the general public (and especially the Inn) at Happystowe had not endowed my father with that Naval rank, and therein confirmed him (in spite of all protest), I might not have got my first invitation, which he cast away like a true Briton. But I leave the world at large, to judge the merits; for I have always found it waste of time to reason with malicious persons.

Have I patience to think of such small fry, when I speak of the greatness of everything at Twentifold Towers, and for miles around? Not a cold, rigid, and stuck-up greatness, such as you must fold your arms to look at, and thank the Lord, in private, that you are not like it; but a warmth of beauty and of kindness shed abroad, which set me on the flutter, when I came to feel it; though my mother had provided me with fifteen pounds of lead, in the hollow at the bottom of my chest. But, at first I was frightened, as you may suppose, and kept asking myself what good would be my best clothes, even to play in, at such a place? Then Lady Twentifold came out, and kissed me, and looked at the tears in my eyes with love—because she had lost a little boy like me—and my heart went to her, so that I saw nothing of the ˑheight or size of any-thing, so long as I could see her, and think about her, and feel how good she was to me.

"You will see a great friend, by and by," she said. "What a distinguished boy you are, to have formed such lofty friendships! And chiefly because of your bodily gift of weighing less than you ought to weigh. Why, a boy, with the mind of a Shakespeare to come, might pour forth poem after poem, and nobody care to inquire into him. Even Professor Megalow, universal as he is, might never even chance to hear of him."

" Oh, is it Professor Megalow ? " I asked, with glad excitement. " I am not afraid of any place, when I know that he is near it."

" Ariel, how unkind of you ! If we illtreat you, spread your wings. But I have not even seen your great friend yet. He will not be here, till dinner-time. He is carving, what he cares for more than anything we can offer—a poor dead whale at Crowton Naze."

Now, behold the reward of virtue—for in the present state of this wicked world, it may be taken as a high reward to escape the pains of punishment! If I had gone, as an Admiral's son, to Twentifold Towers, how should I have looked, when Professor Megalow, knowing all about us, and having smelled our works afar—which probably helped to draw him towards us, for congenial nutriment—now came up, with that large sweet smile, which spreads all over his face and body, and said, " My dear little friend, how are you ? "

This was the first time I ever beheld him in evening dress, and he astonished me; because a very old hat had always been part of his equip-

ment. He may have contrived to leave it some-
where, for he cannot have come with a good one.
Neither was that the only thing in his present
appearance amazing; for he had put himself into
a black velvet coat, as the smartest thing he could
find in his trunk ; and grand, I can tell you, he
looked in it. From daybreak until he had to go
and wash, he had been at work at that great
whale, not only directing a mob of clod-hoppers,
how to hop about upon a whale, but also, with
his own iron arms, performing all work that called
for skill and strength. And yet, there was no sign
of work about him ; neither any talk, or thought
of work ; and he would not be made (though
Lady Twentifold tried her best to make him, and
so did Sir Roland with downright " fishers "—as
we used to call tapping a master at school, to do
a hard sentence for us), by no manner of means
could he be brought to speak, as if he wanted to
be listened to.

This was the very thing that I had known, ever
since he first came, with the other four Professors.
Of them there was not one that would leave off
talking, for the sake of the public, or of one

another, or even for his own sake ; neither
would they breathe enough, to let another voice
in ; but the measure of every man's mind was
his lungs. And to countervail this, it has been
laid down by nature, that the men who have
something to say don't say it.

But, though this Professor, in his leisure time,
would play round the edge of his learning, rather
than plunge other people into it ; it was quite
impossible for even me (a careless, and light-
headed boy) to be with him, without learning
something. And my firm belief is, that although
I know very little, at this time of writing, whatever I have learned of larger things than little
human creatures, was gained upon that whale,
where the great mind came to study the great
body.

CHAPTER XIII.

WHALEBONES.

My dear mother always says, and allows no contradiction about it, that this whale, being all bones and blubber, had no right whatever to come ashore there, and to set me against my father's trade. She declares that all science is full of smells, a thousand times worse than we make; and that all their fuss about drains is just, that they may get themselves cleaned up, for nothing. All the people before her, in generation, lived to be ninety, without any drain upon them; except her own parents, and why did they die? Why, because there was a drain carried through their garden; and the smell came in, and choked them!

In support of this view, there is much to be

said; and according to my own experience, ten people are killed, by the making and opening of drains, for one who can hope in his lungs, that he breathes better air when near them. Nature has designed the human race, to stand well apart on the face of the earth, and not huddle up in hillocks, as the emmets do; and their certainty of fighting, when they get too thick, shows this, without further argument. And another thing that proves it, is the fact, that when they clot together, they make drains; which destroy everybody who is fond of them. My father was as well as any man could be, till what they call "sanitary engineering" broke his constitution; and the lively smells, that our works had scattered, were bottled into deadly poison.

As yet, I was too young to understand such matters, or even to give a thought to them; but the standing I took upon that whale, and the pleasure with which I went into him, did a great deal for me, in the good opinion (than which there could be no better one) of the kind Professor Megalow. Roly would not come anigh our operations, after one experiment, and a short

one; but I, with my quickness and lightness of
tread, was of some little service, I do believe, in
the cause of harmless science. I learned all the
names of the Professor's tools, and could bring
them to him, without wanting any ladder; and
any little cut, that could be made without much
strength, I could make under his direction,
while he was at the bigger work. He did not
attempt to get all the skeleton, greatly as he
longed to do so; for this was no whale to be
found every day, but one who had no business
here; and his name was something like choco-
late. The Professor sighed heavily; as his
bones grew more, and more, attractive, and
hung over us, like a great arbour drooped with
a fine lot of creepers; but he knew, long since,
what it is to depend, for money, upon the
Government. Lucky would he be, to get the
head, and fins, and tail, and some odds and
ends, if a dozen rival claimants would let him
have so much.

"That whale is mine," said Lady Twentifold;
"he chose to land on my property, and I give him
to Professor Megalow; not to the Government,

that won't pay a penny, but to the Professor, to put in his own garden."

"That whale belongs to me," said the local receiver of the droits of the Admiralty; "the foreshore is vested in the Crown, and the Admiralty represents the Crown."

"Clearly, there can be no question," said the man, who represented the Trinity House, "that the whale is ours; and we mean to have him."

Then there came a lawyer, employed by the crew of the boat who had first harpooned him; and another retained by the men who stuck him last; and another by a captain who had espied him go down; and another by a fisherman who headed him ashore; and one by the Coast-guard, who had seen him stranded first; and two by a man who had foretold the weather, and kept his ropes ready, though he never had to use them. But, in spite of all these claims, the men who got him, or at least got all the best of him, were the men who made no claim at all; but came down, with carts and casks, and helped themselves.

For my part, I thought it not only unjust, but stupid, that I should work so hard, and establish a right, as the Professor said, to a very considerable share of blubber, and my father not get a pailful! I wrote to him, beginning with a line of Latin—not so much to accredit my learning, as to make him pay proper attention,—and after that, I said that here there was any quantity of stuff, such as he could never get, for love or money, (unadulterated), and it was to be had, for the asking; or rather for taking, without asking. I told him, how it shone in the sun, and held together, and took different colours as you looked at it; and I was sure that he would make his fortune; because he could get it for nothing, and make it mix up into everything. And I was certain of stirring him up, and getting five shillings, by return of post, when I added—"Everybody says that Mr. Barlow, of Happystowe candle-works, will make a thousand pounds, out of this poor whale, that is being cut up by me, and Professor Megalow."

My mother was kind enough to answer; but without any sort of reference to business. My father took no more notice of my letter, than if I had sent him a bark of *Grip's*, instead of a pill-box, filled with sample from my own knife, at a place where the blubber was more than fourteen inches thick. And this goes some way to prove, that his mind was already on the rise above the smaller details, and getting into larger views of lofty subjects, such as chemical researches, political œconomy, and even Government contracts. And it turned out afterwards, as you will see, that he was right in attending to these wholesale sizes.

Dear mother sent me half a crown in stamps, for fear of my changing the half-sovereign, and related a beautiful dream she had enjoyed, about me, and Professor Megalow, standing on the whale, with our wings spread out. "She knew, from all the pictures, what a whale was like, and hoped (for the sake of my new overcoat) I kept out of the way, when he spouted. And, if I could bring a piece of genuine bone, for the sake of her stays, it would be such a comfort, for everything now was adulterated; and their want of spring ran into her. And then, she added, that she did not think I had better write a line to Polly Windsor (though she sent me a message from Polly, to say that I ought to have done it long ago), because it was not so well to go too far, and create expectations, which might come to nothing. Her own opinion was, that after my last fly, and the high society it led to, there was no telling what might be before me, in the family way, and otherwise. But above all, she begged me, for her dear sake, not to trust to the grand dinners I got here, and their turtle and their venison, and their Aspic jelly, but to keep the tongue of the buckle of my lead-belt in the third hole from the end; for, if the wind took me, out over the sea, what could Lady Twentifold, and the whale, and even the great Professor do?"

I was quite content to save fingers from pen, in the direction of Polly Windsor. Polly was very well in her way; when she chose to be pleased, and look pretty. Moreover, she was a very well-grown girl, with broad shoulders, and big arms, and long brown hair, and her feet so truly a pair, that she never could tell her right shoe from her left. And from her mother she had inherited so much strength of dignity, that, if I went to kiss her, when the mood was not in liking, or if she saw me trying it with any of her enemies, she would take me up with one hand, and lay me on the cinders. But I must not say too much of that; or Sir William Chumps will be down upon me.

We had promised to marry one another; ever since she had her first pink slips, and I went into trousers; but I never vowed not to speak to any other girl, nor to let her box my ears, and say "thank you, dear;" as she seemed to believe that I had done. And surely, it is no great reproach upon me, that now, in this busy time, I never thought about her, unless I got something very good to suck, and wished that she were there to have a bit. For it must be understood, that Professor Megalow, could not do a good stroke of work without me, according to the very best of my belief; and as he was lodging at Crowton Naze, which was more than three miles from the Towers, and as he must get to work, the moment that the sunlight came over the sea into the wattles of the whale, there was no help for it, but that I must be up, by the crow of a

cock, who lived under my window; for not a
serving man, or ruling woman, at the Towers,
would take sixpence a day, to get up so soon.
Sir Roland called me a confounded fool, and
said that I came there to play, and not to work;
and even Lady Twentifold was vexed with me.
But, like everybody else, she fell under the
enchantment of the Professor's eyes, and smile.
And I did hear my lady's favourite maid
declaring to her cousin, who had to make my
bed, that "you should have seen my lady's face,
when she was told, by a friend who pretended to
know all about him, that the Professor had been
married, for several years."

At any rate, he worked as hard, as if he had
a large small family to keep; and I was told
afterwards, and can well believe (because he
was under the Government) that he would have
been paid, more than twice as much, if he had
done less than half the work. But neither of us
gave a thought to that. Our object was to walk
off with the whale, or so much of him as was
moveable; before the twelve lawyers, who were
hard at work, could get an order from the

Courts, to stop us. And luckily, this was the season of the year, when the law (like a Python) retires for three months, to digest its swallowings. Moreover, when a boat's crew of people, (who care for the law, about as much as science does) that is to say, blunt fishermen came with intention of landing at high water, and storming the whale, who was well drawn up,—even the Professor could not have stopped them (though Lady Twentifold's bailiff was there, to back him up, through thick and thin), if once those fellows could have landed. By saying to *Grip* "have a care, my boy," I was able to do a good turn to our cause; for he knew a gun better than I did, and feared no other thing on earth, but that. One look into the boat convinced him that these rogues had got no fire-arms; and as soon as he had knocked over two, who desired to land, the rest held parley.

"Our coast-guard will be withdrawn, next week," the Professor assured them, in his kind and solid way; and whether they misunderstood his meaning, and believed the Preventive men to be in possession, or whether they were glad of some good reason for withdrawal; at any rate they withdrew as promptly, as every one of English race does now, when it might prove troublesome to go on. Moreover, they showed a grand contempt for us; which the mere act of running away exhibits. And in all probability they were wise; for *Grip* had struck back upon ancestral qualities, as some few Englishmen do, even yet. By slow, and solid holding of his own, he had thrashed all the Twentifold Tower dogs, every one of whom was to have eaten him; and now he was living on whalebone, and every muscle was as hard as wire. If mental analogy counts for aught, against low physical resemblance, *Grip* was far more akin to the English race, than the present generation is.

The Professor was delighted with all these works; and, as soon as we had finished, and packed up the results, he laid his hand upon my head. Upon his own, he had a velvet cap; and the whole of his face was one sweet smile.

" Tommy," he said, looking steadfastly at me, and swinging a little from side to side, for he always stood with his head well back, and his heels a trifle forward; "what a help you have been, my dear little Tommy—a truly strong-siding champion! Now, before I go, to see your good works stowed away in our dark recesses, tell me what I can do for you, to show the gratitude of the nation." He was fond of talking in this style, making small things great, and great things small.

"If you please, sir," I said, after thinking awhile, for I believed that he could do anything; "I should be so glad, if you could stop me, from having to go up in the air so."

Professor Megalow's bright smile changed into a smile of sadness. He began to rub his well-established nose, in the fork of his finger and thumb; and then he whistled, and put his hands into his trouser pockets.

"Oh yes, sir, you can, if you like;" I said, taking hold of one thumb, which he had left out; "there is nothing of the things that can be done, that you can't do, when you like, sir. I only want to be able to take off this lead, that makes me blue all round, and to leave these heavy things behind; and get to feel the ground

under my feet go firm; as it seems to do, with
everybody else but me. I have longed so often
to ask you, sir ; but I did not like, until you
asked me. Oh, Sir Megalo-micro-sauros, do try
to help me, if I have helped you."

He had told me to call him " Micro-sauros "
once, when I stuck fast with his proper name,—
" for our origin now is established, my Tommy ;
and yet, we may modify our pedigrees. My
proclivities show me to be devolved, in a very
degenerate, and underfed form, from the mighty
race of Saurians." And as cause, and effect,
interlace each other, he spent his life, in dis-
secting his ancestors.

" Thomas," he said now, for whenever he
spoke in a very solid vein, he called me that;
" Thomas, my boy, be contented with that,
which has been ordained concerning you. Yours
is not the only instance of what our friends call
Meiocatobarysm ; the meaning of which you have
Greek enough now, as well as experience enough
to know. The form of life, in which you find
yourself, is perhaps the happiest among all, with
which we are as yet acquainted—to wit, that of

an English boy, of the middle class, well-fed,
well-taught, well-played (if I may be allowed the
expression), dressed, quite as well as he cares
to be, and walking about at his leisure, with an
eye down the manifold vistas of mischief. In a
few years, Thomas will have changed all that.
He will find himself bound to pay rates, and
taxes, and never know when he has paid them
right; to go to his office, with a compressor on
his head, and measure his words, like poison :
to doubt his very oldest friends, and be hearty
with people he can't bear the sight of ; and to go
home at night, with the certainty that one run
of bad luck may ruin him. Thomas, be happy
while you can."

"But, sir," I answered ; "how can I be happy,
when everybody expects me to go up ? No one
else, in the world, is expected to go up ; because
he couldn't do it, if he tried. And I can't go up,
more than once in a way ; even if my mother
would allow me. And yet, I am always getting
blamed, by a number of people, for not going
up. Even Roly is down upon me now, to do
it ; and because I won't try, but keep work-

ing at the whale, he seems to be getting tired
of me."

"Tommy, that is sad; and yet a natural
result. To my far less remarkable self, it has
happened; when kind friends expected me to rise
too fast. Reserve yourself, Tommy; and preserve your self-respect. But would you be really
glad, my boy, to lose this special gift of yours?
Remember, that if you do, you cease to attract
any public attention—doubtful benefit as that
may be. Do you really wish, to be unable to
pirouette in the air again?"

Professor Megalow, in the kindest manner,
put both hands on my shoulders, and fixed his
very large clear eyes on mine. It was hopeless
for any one, looked at thus, to tell a lie; neither
was my nature that.

"If you please, sir," I said, "there is nothing
I like better, than to be taken for a wonder of
the world, and to read a whole column in the
Newspapers about me, beginning with 'Unparalleled phenomenon.' But what I can't bear
is, to be always bothered to do it, for people to
look at; and to be laughed at, as if I were a

rogue, or else a curmudgeon, when I don't go
up, to order. Sometimes, I have been tempted
to pull my weights off—but I promised my
mother, that I never would do that. And you
know, sir, that I can only go up, now and then;
and always, when I don't want to do it. And
when I come down again, I am so stupid; and
my head goes round, for hours."

"The natural result of anything counter to
the ordinary laws of earth. Have you anything
more to explain, concerning your wishes, so far
as you know them?"

"No, sir, except that I should like once, to go
up, if it was only as high as his hat, when my
father was there, to see me do it. Because he is
so cock-sure that I can't do it; and he calls it
nothing but a pack of lies. And, somehow or
other, I assure you, sir, I am just like a lump
of lead, when father is looking at me."

"A common complaint of the *Mediums*,
Tommy, of the effect incredulity has on them.
But, my dear little anthropic nautilus, I can do
nothing, either to make, or mar your excursions
over my own head. As I have told you before,

there is nothing exceptional in your formation ;
only it happens, that your bodily contour is
exactly such as to promote the tendencies of
your specific levity. Do you understand me,
noble volant ?"

" Well, sir, I think that I do a little ; but not
very clearly, until I get older. Bodily contour
means the turning of my body, when I go up ;
doesn't it ? "

" No, Tommy, no. It means physical outline ;
if that is any clearer to you. You give me a
lesson in lucidity, as the cant of the day calls
clearness. To put what I mean, into the vulgar
tongue—which is the least vulgar of all just
now—your outward shape is especially fitted, to
help the lightness of your material, in conquering
the power of gravitation. Your chest is very
large, and can be much expanded ; your head is
rather small, and of little substance, but endowed
with a mass of curls, which take the wind, like
a mop being trundled ; your feet are very hollow
and receive the air ; and the palms of your hands
are concave. Above all, your stomach, my dear
little friend, or rather your hypogastrium, has a

curve, which requires continual attention, in the
way of aliment. If neglected, this lends itself
at once to inferior pressure. But with all these
qualifications, Tommy, you might defy the
breezes, if you only had a stable mind, and
bones a little more like mine."

The Professor had goodly bones of his own,
as behoves a great osteologist; whereas mine
are very small, and slight, and it takes some
time to find them. But I saw no way to
increase their size; and before I could ask, if
such there were, Sir Roland came cantering up,
and behind him appeared his mother, in a pony-
carriage, together with her lovely child, Miss
Laura.

" Oh, how we shall miss you !" exclaimed my
dear lady—as I was allowed to call her—"Professor Megalow, if I establish my right to the
residue of that whale, I shall have it preserved,
and a gallery made, in gratitude for all that we
have learned from you."

" I heartily hope that you will," he replied,
gracefully lifting his velvet cap, as he always
did at a compliment; " then there will be some

excuse, for me to come down, and have another carve at him."

"Professor," cried Sir Roland, who was always wanting something; "there is one thing that you must do, before you go, for the finishing touch to our gratitude. You must send Tommy up, in this nice quiet reach, without any fellow here to shoot at him; and we'll tie this kite-string to his belt, after we have taken the lead out; to make sure of his not drifting out to sea."

"Tommy, and I, are very warm allies," my great friend answered gravely; "and unless you behave most respectfully to him, I shall tie the kite string to you, and with her ladyship's permission, send up you."

That was a very fine moment for me, who have been compelled by my peculiar case, to keep such a sharp look-out, what all the people around me are thinking of. In every condition of things, even my best friends have always considered it a nice little piece of excitement, and a pleasure entirely due to them, that I should go up, and encounter all risk, while they remained below, with the heartiest wishes for my safe deliverance.

Sir Roland Towers-Twentifold looked at the Professor, as if to say, at first, " You could not do it, if you tried." The Professor regarded him, with earnest sadness, as much as to say— " Don't make me try; because it might be so bad for you." Then Roly, in doubt and alarm, glanced towards his mother; who had said that he knew no fear. Her eyes were saddened with a gleam of tears, for she had long made up her mind, that the great Professor could do anything permitted by the laws of England. Yet honour, and fine sentiment, forbade her to forbid, that her son should do a thing, which he had urged a friend to do. The wise man enjoyed the situation for a moment; then perceived that it was painful to kind and good friends, and at once relieved them.

" I withdraw my proposal, which was rashly made;" he said to Lady Twentifold, with that wonderful mixture of nod and wink, which had neither nod in it, nor wink, perceptible, and yet conveyed the force of both; " I am truly glad, that I did not give your dauntless son time to accept my offer. Perhaps it would have puzzled me, if he had. Especially as my train will be due in an hour, and the drive to the Station takes forty minutes. Is there any gratitude, in the sons of men? If there be, how little time have I left to express it—and yet the wisest plan; for no length of time would suffice me!"

He lifted her white hand to his lips, in the gallant manner, which became him well; and my dear lady bowed over it, and turned to her carriage, with a little sigh, which conveyed to the ponies—if they understood their mistress— that it was through no default of hers, that they never would be guided by a strong male hand.

CHAPTER XIV.

A SILLY PAIR.

I HAVE often been taunted, by people who know
nothing (multiplied into a million fibs) about
me, that my mind is as volatile as my body, and
goes about, in an unsettled manner, for want of
the leaden belt, which motherly care so long
kept round my stomach.   It is equally needless,
and useless, to present reason to such irrationals;
and I try to be proud, in my loftier moments, of
affording them amusement, which amuses me.

But, to reasonable persons, who can hearken
to a thing, and take it into common sense, and
weigh it—whenever it concerns their own affairs
enough—to these (if any) I would simply say,
" follow my own history of my own acts, and
judge, by my own account, of what nobody else

can know so well." And any one, proceeding
upon this fair principle, will find more to approve
than to condemn in me, however much I may
tell against myself.

Hoping that fair-play will prevail—as it generally does in the end—I confess, that at this
very tender age of fifteen, I proved for the rest
of my holidays, untrue to the image of Polly
Windsor. Polly was not there; and even if she
had been, how would she have looked, I should
like to know, by the side of Laura Twentifold?
She was double her size, that is certain at the
least; but in quality, oh what a difference!
And yet again, manners, and the fear of what
I might say greatly against my own interest,
enable me to speak in a chastened style; and
to do that, I had better leave Polly still absent.

On the very day after Professor Megalow returned to his duties in London, my dear lady
comforted her mind, by returning to the place
still full of him. You must understand, that
the Professor had never been actually staying at
the Towers; because, without any other full-
grown gentleman dwelling in the house, it might

have looked amiss. So he had his own camping place at Crowton-on-the-Naze, which is ten miles further up the coast than the rising watering-place, called Happystowe. Yet there had not been many days, when he failed to put himself into spruce attire—so far as his nature permitted—and to dine, and make a pleasant evening, with my lady, and her gallant son, Sir Roland. And when he was gone, it could not be helped, that the evenings should grow long, and dull.

It must have been August, and about the middle of it (according to our holidays, which were sadly near their end), when my dear Lady walked down the sands, to talk to an ancient fisherman, about keeping the relics of the whale upright. Roly was gone, with the Keeper, inland, to see about exercising some young dogs, in preparation for the shooting-time; and the lovely little lady, and myself, were left, to look for pretty shells, and to amuse each other. And I never grew tired of obeying her commands; so sweet was her voice, and so gentle were her eyes.

"Now I want to show all these," she said, "to my darling Dorothea, that she may choose exactly what she likes; and it is high time to put her necklace on, that you have made so beautifully, Ariel."

She always called me "Ariel;" because she had heard her mother do it, once or twice, and she said it was so much prettier than "Tommy." And although she was more than ten years old, she had not outgrown the wholesome joy of a little woman in her baby-doll. Dorothea, moreover, was quite young at present, and sweetly instructive in the newest fashions, having only come two days ago from Paris, with the kind introduction of Professor Megalow.

"You may sit down quite close to dear Dorothea; because you are not clumsy and rough, like Roly; who cannot at all enter into the feelings of a lovely and delicate creature, like this. And, Ariel, I am quite sure that Dolly will like you, as soon as she opens her eyes, which are shut now—you must understand—from the sea-air being too much for her. But you must let me put her necklace on, although you have made it so beautifully ; not that I would not trust you to do it, but because you cannot understand her hair. It would hardly be proper, if you did, you know."

She was always like this, such a sweet little love ; so afraid of hurting anybody's feelings, and so ready to think everybody good. When I sat down near her, on a bank of bed-rushes, with the doll sitting carefully between us, I could not help feeling ungrateful in my heart, for the prospect of Miss Polly Windsor to-morrow. And I could not quite fancy that Maiden Lane—though alive with delights of its proper class—could supply such contentment to sight, and thought (not that I put it so grandly then) as the place I sate in, and the things I saw. For the tide was coming in, with pleasant feeling of the air, and ready briskness of the things, that had been waiting for it. At every short step that it made in advance—for the waves toddled in, like babies—there was some pretty thing, starting up in front, to run, and to glisten before it. But the prettiest thing of all sate there by me.

"You are always at work," she said, "always doing something. Why do people want us to be educated so? Those funny letters are all Greek, I know; because Roly has got some that he learns at Harrow. But he doesn't seem to like it, more than I like French; and he puts it in a cupboard, for the holidays. Ariel, why should you work more than Roly does? He never does a thing, unless he likes it."

I had thought this out, and my reply was ready. "Roly will be a rich man, and I shall not. He belongs to great people, and I belong to small ones. He will get on all the same, whether he works, or not."

"Then I call that as unfair as anything can be. And I could not have believed it, though I know you tell the truth, unless I had heard of such things before. We all ought to work, to do good, of course; but not in the middle of the holidays."

"I have got to go back to old Rum, on Monday;" I answered, with a wistful gaze at her; "and unless I can say a hundred lines of Homer, beginning at the place where we left off, cracks

will be the word, and no mistake. And he's
come to be so sharp, from being done so often,
that there's not a fellow now with the pluck to
run a tib, or a crib, or a leary round the
corner. *Ton d' apameibomenos* is the only cock
that fights."

"What a lucky thing it is to be a girl!" She
cast her eyes down, after looking at me, to learn
my opinion of this sentiment; for that opinion
showed itself as opposite as could be, to hers.
"I only mean because we don't get cracks, and
we don't jump on one another, as they do to
you sometimes; oh, Ariel, how can you put up
with that? And then they tie a string to your
toe at night. What courage it must take, to be
a boy!"

"Before Bill Chumps went to Oxford," I replied, while looking at the tiny foot, she put forth
on the sand; "he shut up all bullying, in our
school. There used to be a lot of it; and
after getting taw, or togy, in the playground,
and rats in school, a fellow couldn't sleep, for
fear of cramp. But Bill set up a different
fashion altogether; and the little fellows now

begin to cock over us, who are their seniors. I
am getting bigger than I used to be, and so well
up in the school, that I am very useful, in doing
the big fellows' exercises. And they never jump
on me, as they used to do, when I couldn't try
to fly for them. *Grip* would have something to
say to them, next morning, if they tried it."

" Oh, I do love *Grip*, because he is so ugly ;
and I love you, Ariel, because you are so pretty,
and so kind, and gentle ; and you never do mischief, unless Roly sets you the example. I shall
cry, when you go away ; I'm sure I shall ; and
I shall put Dorothea into mourning for you. I
don't believe a bit that your papa makes candles ;
and if he does—how could we go to bed, without
them ? I should just like to ask people that.
And what could they say, I should be glad to
know ? "

To me this appeared an extremely sensible,
and large-minded view of the case, and I did not
hesitate to promote it.

" And what would you do without soap, Lady
Laura ? My father makes soap of the finest
quality. A great deal better, as everybody says,

than any turned out by Mr. Windsor, though he put his name on every cake—'Windsor's best brown Windsor.' And no better than curds, every square of it."

"Then if I see any of it in my room, I shall throw it straight out of the window, and say 'Please to bring me Ariel's soap.' But you must not call me 'Lady Laura.' My mother is a lady, but I am not; till I marry my cousin, Lord Counterpagne; as they say I shall have to do, when I grow up. But I don't care about him at all, till then. He has got red hair, and his eyes are crooked."

Although it was no concern of mine, this arrangement appeared to me most unfair. But I did not dare to say a word against it.

"Oh, Ariel," my little beauty went on, after taking up her doll, and coaxing it; "can you think of anything so bad, as marrying a person you don't like? Because you can never get away, you know; according to the law of the land, I believe, and according to the Bible. My mother has never said a word about it; but Roly declares that I am bound to do it, and he

is always determined to have his own way. Oh,
Dorothea, what would you do?"

I knew very little of the world as yet, and in
matters above me, I was loth to speak; but I
could not help saying—"There is lots of time
yet. You may trust me to help you, if you
only let me know."

"How stupid I am! I never thought of that;"
she turned over towards me, and put up her
hands, as if for me to help her; and then
suddenly began to stroke my hair, as she had
often longed to do, but had hitherto refused my
invitation. "I must do it once, before you go,
to see how the whole of it is fastened on. Don't
be afraid; I won't hurt you, Ariel. I know how
Ethel Jones does mine. And if they want to
marry me, and I don't like it, all you will have
to do, is this—to get into the train, and come
down here, and then take off your lead, and fly
away with me, and come back when the cere-
mony is over."

"But how could they do it, without you?" I
asked.

"You musn't expect me to be reasonable

always;" she answered, and began to play with
me, gently, and beautifully, and laughing all the
time.

"What a pair of silly little things you are!"
Lady Twentifold came upon us suddenly, while
Laura was trying to uncurl my hair, and I was
offering to kiss her, but afraid to do it; while
she was dodging in and out, to tempt me more;
"Ariel, you told me this morning, that unless
you learned a hundred lines of Greek to-day,
you had better not be born, next Monday. And
you asked me to write a letter of apology, to
your learned Dr. Rumbelow. He is likely to
be our new Bishop, I was told this morning;
and it will put Roly down, for he made sure that
his Master would receive the offer. So I hope
that you will never call him 'Old Rum,' any
more."

"Old Rum to be the Bishop, my dear lady!"
I cried, as if I had quite lost my place. "And
who is to be our master, I should like to know?
Oh, I won't learn another line; 'twould be trouble
thrown away."

My practical conclusion was borne out by

facts—sad facts for all sons of the *Partheneion*.
Dr. Rumbelow's luck was a joy to us, at first;
because we all liked him, and got off a lot of
work. But our joy soon went, and a bad time
followed; as we all found out, and pretty quickly
too. For the new master's name, was Crankhead, "Ernest Mauleverum Crankhead," M.A.,
a Cambridge man, and a lofty Wrangler; but
without much Greek, as we soon found out.

Now, before I left Twentifield Towers, and
returned to the smell of our works,—which had
changed very greatly for the worse, while I was
away down here,—Sir Roland Towers-Twentifold (being well sixteen, and tall for his age, and
of long experience, at one of our largest public
schools) took me aside into a saddle-room, wherein
he was learning to smoke cigars, and put into a
nutshell all the essence of the British Constitution. How I wish, I could remember what he
said! But it sank into my mind, too deeply
ever to be brought up again; and it blended
with, and flourished in, the flower of my life;
as liquid manure reappears in bright flowers,
" *inscripti nomina regum.*"

"Tommy," he went on, as soon as ever he had put into ten words the lessons of a thousand years, "you will see now, how it is that we don't get on. We never get a man to take the lead, who knows his own mind, and will stick to it, and throw up his situation, rather than carry it on, against his own lights. And then, there come a lot of fellows swarming for first pull, as we rush to the swipes-can after cricket; and the louder any cad is for his rights (which are sure to mean the wrongs of some quieter chap), the surer he is to get served first. Now, can you call this Government ?"

"I don't pretend to know much about it," I replied, for we had held some conversation of this kind before; "but my father says, that any business carried on, as the Government of this country is, would have to put its shutters up, within three months, if it started with a hundred thousand pounds. But you mustn't tell any one that he said this; for I believe, by the way he would not answer me, that he has got a fine Government contract, by this time."

"Your father is quite right; he is a man of

strong sense;" Sir Roland made answer, as soon
as he could, after taking a large puff of smoke
the wrong way; "let him get every farthing he
can from the Government, and then he will be
able to understand them. Why, I might not
have got the knowledge that I have, except
for a trick that they wanted to play about my
cousin Counterpagne, when he comes of age.
Counterpagne is soft, and his mother no better;
and being of an ancient Tory race, they expected
to have things made smooth for them. But I
can't stop, to tell you all that now. You are to
come back at Christmas, and you shall hear it
then. Counterpagne is to marry little Laura,
to prevent any mischief to our property, and
influence; and between us, we shall send six
members up, besides Counterpagne himself in
the Peers of course, and me in the Commons, for
the Towers' own hole. But, Tommy, look at
me, and tell me this. If under a Government,
that calls itself Conservative, as the present
fellows do, such things can be done, as I was
going to tell you; what is to be expected of the
Radicals? I'll tell you what; if the Constitu-

tion lasts till I am of age, which seems a most unlikely thing—I shall want you, and every man of sense I know, to collect, and put your shoulders to the wheel. Remember that."

I did not at all understand what he meant, although he had spoken several times to this effect. But I promised to do all I could ; and was pleased with the thoughts of becoming so important.

"Tommy, you will rise," my friend continued, without asking what I was thinking of : " such a fellow as you are, must go up, unless he makes a downright fool of himself. You can beat me all to fits, in Greek and Latin, though you have only been at a dirty little private school. You have got a most wonderful face of your own ; so easy-going, and sweet-tempered, that it makes every fellow think you slow, and drop all jealousy about you. And more than all,—and that alone should be enough to make your fortune—you can draw the attention of the whole world upon you. whenever you please, by going over their heads. I have been very good, in letting you off, without sending you up, a lot of times. But you know

that I have done it upon one condition—you
must cultivate the art, without any one's knowledge, and be ready to go up, at some great
moment, when I give the signal. Pretend, for
the present, that you can't do it; but practise, as
I told you, more and more. I have shown you
the muscles you must try to strengthen, and
the places where you must lay on fat. It is
nothing in the world, but a kind of swimming;
and there everything depends upon your being
quite at home. Now, remember what I say;
and when you come down at Christmas, I shall
put you through your paces, and expect to find
you perfect."

"Oh, Roly," I replied, "you talk as lightly
as all the men of science did about me. I will
do my very utmost to please you, I am sure.
But I never expect to be of any service to you.
You are learning to smoke, and your smoke goes
up; and that makes you think that I can do the
same."

"Exactly so, Tommy. A great deal of it went
down, until I understood it. And now look at
that!"

CHAPTER XV.

POLITICAL ŒCONOMY.

By going from home, after so many years, we
had not only done ourselves no good—in the
opinion of our friends, who could not go—but
we had opened the door to a swarm of changes,
which came rushing in upon the heels of each
other. To me, the greatest change of all appeared to have taken place in Maiden Lane
itself; for the houses had turned black, and
the windows grimy, and the roadway and the
pavement (wherever there was any) seemed to
cry aloud for washing, and the people too, un-
conscious as they were of such desire.

Excitement appeared to be the main thing
now, and hurry, and suspicion, and no **time**
to look about; whereas both at Happystowe, and

Crowton-on-the-Naze, the chief business of the natives was, to look at one another; and when there was no more to be made of that, to consider the meaning of the sand and sea. And taken on the whole, those folk looked wiser, and a great deal happier than ours did.

But to dwell upon that, would be ungraceful now, when I call to mind that our own boiling, and the agitation of my father's engine had a great deal to do with the ferment around us. No sooner had my father returned to business —with Joe Cowl, and the summons, wiped off his conscience, and Billy Barlow's new devices written in his heart—than he found on his desk, he could never tell how, a sealed invitation to tender for soap, for the heads of all the convicts (with average stated), in six great castles, for the improvement of our race. The consumption of soap, per head was given, and a number of smaller particulars, all in print and proper columns; and then the requirement for samples, to be delivered at six places. And in pencil, very faint upon the margin, there was written, "It must not be soft, and it must be strong. Price

not to be too low, like the Rads' stuff. Tallow
will be wanted soon. *Rub this out.*" There
was something so touching in this, and so full
of fine feeling, as between man and man, that
my father immediately filled his pipe, and had
a good smoke to consider it. At one time, his
heart warmed up with thinking of the goodwill
remaining in politics yet, and the loyalty every
one is bound to show to, and expect from, his
own side. And yet again, he could not feel sure,
that he ought to have any faith at all in this.
Why should there be six samples sent, of a
stone weight each, to six different places, and
all to be left without the money? It looked like
a hoax, with Joe Cowl at the root of it, to get
a paltry laugh at him ; or else a swindle, to get
three-fourths of a hundredweight of soap, for
nothing. He resolved to act warily, and so he
did. "If they mean well to me," he said, "they
will never examine my samples."

They meant so thoroughly well to him, that
they sniffed at his samples, and found them
shocking—for he sent the worst stuff he could lay
hand on, for fear of having it stolen—and then

they gave an order for sixty tons, to be furnished at once, and sixty more to follow. Our works had never sent out such a lot before, at one delivery; and no wonder that they could not think of me.

"John Windsor shall not have a finger in the pie;" my father said right manfully; "I am not at all sure that his politics are sound. He would lower my quality, to get the next himself. You know how he wanted to run away, Sophy, when that great bombardment came. Let every vat stand upon its own bottom."

"Bucephalus, you are quite right," mother answered; "as you always are, when you get on. Work double tides, Bubbly, and double your hands. Don't let them have a penny, if you can help it."

So grand was the commodity thus produced, with the help of the lessons at Happystowe, that it is remembered to the present day, and cited as the type of excellence. For sanitary purposes it was needed; and it not only met but transcended them. There was not a convict left with a stub of hair, though their hair is always

bristly; and very few had such constitution,
as to keep any roots for future trouble. Universal satisfaction was expressed, and my father
put up the Royal Arms, twice as big as the
knacker's across the road, and done in thicker
timber. "Thoroughly candid, and straight-forward," he said to every one who spoke of it;
"good value for money, good money for value.
Public confidence met, by private industry,
enterprise, and honour. I serve them exactly
as I should serve you. Just to turn five per
cent. on my money, and no more. If any man
calls that exorbitant, let him come and do it
cheaper."

The only thing at all mysterious was the
requirement for six samples, to be delivered
at six places far apart. But that was explained
most pleasantly, so that my father rubbed his
hands, and chuckled, while he was reading the
debates, in the early part of the following
session. A figuresome member of the Oppo-
sition, who thought himself fit to be Chancellor
of the Exchequer, had given notice of a question, concerning a certain contract for soap, to

be supplied to Her Majesty's penal establish-
ments, etc., with dates, and other insinuations.
And he made a very hasty speech about it, con-
founding the *post*, and the *propter hoc ;* quite
as if my father, whom he dared to call a
"wholly unknown manufacturer," had been pre-
ferred for a lucrative contract, because of his
behaviour at election-time ! So far as wicked-
ness can be good, this man spoke well, having
got up all his facts ; and he sate down in
triumph, as he thought.

But before he had time to digest his cheers,
the gentleman, who was to reply got up, with
a beautiful smile, and a very pleasant glance
at a paper laid before him. "I am furnished
with particulars, from the head of the depart-
ment, concerning this heinous transaction, sir,"
he said ; "and I find that large samples were
delivered in six quarters, widely apart, and
wholly unconnected ; the names of which I will
read, if desired." Loud cheers followed from
every corner of the House—for nobody likes to
have his own rights interfered with—and the
speaker concluded. "I will ask for no apology.

From the Honourable Member for Clap-trap, it would be of no more value than his imputation."

"Well," said my father, when he had read this twice; "I call that something like a Government. If we only get a few more contracts, Sophy, we'll send Tommy into the House, to see about them. There might be a stranger thing, my dear, than a long blue paper for ten thousand pounds, with " Thomas Upmore" signed for Her Majesty above, and " Bucephalus Upmore," for himself below. What a rage John Windsor will be in, when he reads about those six samples, and not one of them gone out of his gate! I had sense enough to keep the whole of that inside my own waistcoat."

Now, it would have been good, and even pleasant for the public—lustily though they condemned us, at the time—if the only increase of activity shown in those parts had come out of our chimneys. But there always is a mob of people, who never will leave well alone; and these had got up deputations, petitions, memorials, circulars, indignation meetings, committees, commissions, and worst of all missiles, concerning

the wholesome smell we made, and had made
before some of their fathers were born. When
the unenlightened mass of minds falls into this
bubonic fever of excitement, the right thing to
administer is gruel, in the form of general
promises, a desire to hear all that can be said,
and a thoroughly unselfish gratitude towards
those, who have made the worst of you. But
my father had never possessed this wisdom,
which belongs of sweet right to the Liberals;
and whether on the ground of true British principle, or the Royal Arms, or the money coming
in, he took a firm stand, with his hands in his
pockets, and his legs well apart, and defied the
public.

"Every blessed flue of mine," he said, "have
gone ten feet higher, since I were a boy; and
with present foundations, can't go no higher.
Before folk grumble, their place is to stump up.
If every cantankerous fellow, who don't know
a wholesome smell by the touch of it, would
put down a half-crown, if he has got one,
instead of signing lies against me, I don't know
but what I might lay foundations, and change

my insurance, and go twenty foot higher.
Though a heap of disease would break out, I
expect. Look at the plants in my bed-room
window, scarlets, and blue things, and lilies of
the Nile! Is there any man, or woman, round
these parts, half so good-looking, or so sweet
to come by? They like it rarely, and so would
you, if you understood what is good for you.
And who was here first, you, or I, and my
fathers, for three generations of boilers? We
didn't want the houses; they came round us;
every brick of them was laid, with my smoke to
set it. And very good neighbours they have
always been, till this scientific stuff came up,
about cur-bones, and oxen, and the Lord knows
what! I tell you what—if you don't like it,
budge yourself, but you won't budge me."

Such speeches only made the fuss grow
louder; until the authorities felt themselves
compelled to do something sanatory. There
was no " Metropolitan Board of Works," as yet,
I believe; or if there was, it never came up our
way. But the Vestry of St. Pancras had many
stormy meetings, which my father deigned not

to attend; but his workmen were there in great force, and made more noise than our new steam-engine. In short, the matter came (as every matter does now, and the practice already was beginning) to what is called "a reasonable and satisfactory compromise, conciliating all interests." The complaint of the public had been about the air, and the noxious exhalations, and vile odours, as they chose to call them. But who can see the air? Who can tell what is in it? It varies with every puff of wind. Let us turn to something tangible. The earth is a thing that can be dealt with, and the earth is at the bottom of every mischief on the face of it. So, to cure the smell of our chimneys, they ordered a four-foot culvert down our valley, where the course of the old Fleet-stream had been; and the voice of the public went off to it.

This being settled, my father was enabled to make tenfold the smells he had ever made before, without any one hoisting a handkerchief. An inquisitive stranger would sometimes ask, whether this neighbourhood was always choked

with vapours, which he coarsely stigmatized.
A piece of valuable advice, common (yet neglected universally) about the prior claims of
his own affairs, was the only reward for his
sympathies. What right had a fellow, with a
walking-stick, to come grumbling against our
rate-payers, and their engineers, and con-
tractors? Measures were being taken, or at
any rate were in contemplation; and every
man with a horse and cart would get fifteen
shillings a day for them.

But alas, how little do we forecast, while we
vindicate, our own welfare! It would have
been better for my dear father—as upright and
downright a man as ever lived—to have gone
to the expense of a new chimney-stack one
hundred feet high, or even to have put out all
his fires, than to have helped to bring that
drain, down our hitherto Maiden valley. The
soil in the bottom was of concentrated essence,
combining all the density of bygone generations
with the volatile relics of their labours. It
would grow almost anything, if only scratched,
and no healthier place for a walk could be

found ; but wisdom is not justified of her fathers, when she goes to turn them up.

In happy ignorance of woes impending, I went back to the *Parthencion*, and found the whole establishment turned upside down. *Grip* came with me, as a thing of course, and found his old barrel standing on its head, and a notice upon it in large letters—"No dogs allowed." If anything rouses the juvenile spirit, such rude breach of prescription does it. With the help of Jack Windsor, who was quite of my mind, I replaced the barrel in its old position, which was snug in a corner impregnable to guns, and I fastened him there with his own long chain, and said, " Now defend yourself, old boy. I have got lots of money, and you shall not starve." He fully understood the situation ; and if any demand for sympathy arose, it would be on behalf of the individual attempting to dislodge him.

Then all of us were summoned to the hall, to hear an oration from the " Principal "—as he styled himself, to start with—our new school-master, Ernest Mauleverum Crankhead, a short

brisk gentleman, quite young, with a pale square
face, a yellow moustache, and very quick bronzy
eyes, which never took two seconds' rest upon
anything. Accustomed as we were to the long
grave countenance, waving white locks, and
calm abstracted gaze of our simple old Dr.
Rumbelow, we could not believe that we saw
the new man; until he stood up at what he
called the *rostrum*, and hit it three times, with
an ivory hammer.

"Going, going, gone!" Jack Windsor whispered; and gone was the glory of the *Partheneion*. We knew it, we felt it, without a word
uttered, our hearts fell into the heels of our
socks; and no boy thought twice of the things
in his pocket. Our account would be with a
sharp hand now, a resolute, and a malignant
one; and what was worst of all, and which a
boy descries at the very first glance,—we should
not have to deal with a gentleman. "I shall
never go up any more," thought I.

I remember very little of what Crankhead
said; and none of it is worth repeating. But
he gave us to understand, that the sooner we

forgot everything we had learned hitherto, and began on lines entirely new, the better it would be for our own minds, and what mattered far more, our success in life. For the few, whose parents might still be benighted enough to insist upon Greek and Latin, a Classical Master would be kept, but the College — for such he had the cheek to call it—would henceforth aim at a loftier mark. Science was the noble, and simple distinction, the all-absorbing element of this age. Mankind had been lying on their backs till now, looking up at the stars, and at imaginary Powers; now they arose, and asserted their rights, and their kinship to every organic being, and the interchangeability of everything. Classes for science would be formed to-morrow, under the charge of the four most eminent Professors of the period, Professors Brachipod, and Jargoon, Chocolous, and Mullicles!

At the sound of their names, these gentlemen appeared. Conscience, and prudence, alike induced me to push Jack Windsor in front of me, because he was both broad and thick.

CHAPTER XVI.

NO EXTRAS.

BEING older now, by several years, than when I had expected to be cut up all alive, and having been taught by Professor Megalow, that science is not of necessity cruel, I managed to sleep pretty well that night, and resolved to be brave in the morning. And truly there was no great need for courage; which rather disappointed me, and cast a slur upon my value, as a boy of exceptional interest. Not one of the four Professors took the trouble to look twice at me; each had his whole time taken up, in fighting for his own tongue, and purse. Their payment was to be by head of pupils—whether they fitted the head, or not—and being four in number, they put universal knowledge into four departments, each with a bigger name than the other. And all our chaps, without ever having heard what the meaning of these big names was, had to put down his own (however short it might be) under sixteen columns, out of thirty-two, headed with the titles of the mysterious studies. Each of the Professors was to take eight sciences, for the subjects of his lectures; and most unfairly we were not allowed to know the human names presiding over each humanity. Every single boy of us wanted to sign to be under Professor Chocolous; not only because (as a general rule) great fun can be had with a German, and he is nearly always easy-tempered, familiar, and kind-hearted; but also because we had heard of his ambition to transmit a nascent tail to his descendants, and what could be finer than to help in its establishment? And next to him, we wanted to be under Mullicles, although about him we knew very little; except that he looked very soft, and expected to be dis-integrated, without notice, into his component particles. On the other hand, Brachipod was as sharp, and full of points, as a cupping instru-

ment; and Jargoon as dry, and creaky with long
words, as a slow steam-roller pounding granite.

With heavy dismay I sate down, and gazed at
the broad sheet laid before me. At the top
were placed alphabetically the names of the
thirty-two sciences proposed; names which
must have been anguish to conceive, agony to
pronounce, and despair to remember. Under
each name was a column, for the hapless victim
to inscribe his own; and at the bottom a
merciful notice—"No pupil need enter for more
than sixteen of the above studies, during the
present term. But all will be expected, in the
ensuing term, to proceed to those which they
now pretermit. The fee for each course of
lectures is one guinea, payable in advance."

Although I could get on with Homer pretty
well, and had read the first book of Herodotus,
and one of "Porson's Four," and some Xeno-
phon, it took me a long time to make out the
name of any one of those sciences. I turned to
my Lexicon, and sought for some, and for
others I hunted in my Latin Dictionary, and
seemed to get near some, but not to be sure;

while of others there was no vestige. I was not aware yet, that the authors of these words are as rash with the Classics, as they are with logic, and maltreat the dead languages, as freely as the living.

"I'll tell you what I'll do," Jack Windsor said; "I'll go in for all thirty-two; and let father stump up, if he's got the blunt for it. Here goes 'John Windsor,' thirty twice over."

What a flood of light those plain words shed on my foggy, and thickly-fibred brain, unwitting as yet of the Athenian prototypes of all the Pansophists, pea for pea, in the pods of Aristophanes! The *blunt* was the point of all points with these hungry professors; and none could be got out of me. And yet, I should never have thought of that, without Jack's plain way of putting it. So I squared my elbow, and sprang my pen, and took care that the ink in it was not too round, and I said, " Don't jerk my elbow, Jack; it is no time for larks of any sort." And then I wrote, in fair hand, across all thirty-two columns, these simple words. " Father don't pay for extras. They tried it on before, but he would not have it. Signed, Thomas Upmore; witness, John Windsor."

This was a bold stroke of mine; and it succeeded, as a bold stroke often does, when it has the force of truth behind it. As soon as all these signatures of zealots for new learning (of whom a great many could not spell their own names) had been received in "Council," by our new Principal, and his four "highly-cultured co-adjutors"—oh Lord, where is good English buried?—there came a squeaky call, from their sacred cell (as different from old Rum's sonorous, "send him hither," as the cry of a mouse behind the wainscot is from the roar of a lion) and the boy who had the longest ears made it out to be —"the presence of Thomas Upmore is required."

Now, I never had any great amount of pluck, which is a steadfast element; while all my elements were light and fleeting, and never would stand up together (as in a fine character they must do) without going up into the air, and turning round. A miserable shiver went through my heart, and turned my bright cheeks to a sad pale blue—so the other fellows said; though it recked me naught what manner of boy I might be, to look at.

"Tommy, keep your pecker up;" Jack Windsor hit me a slap on the back, to impress this counsel, which would have taken all my breath away, if it had not been gone already; "think of your dad, and all the money he is making. Stick well up to them, that's the only ticket. Make them all shake in their shoes, dear Tommy. They will send for me next. If you frighten them well, you will give me pluck to go on with it."

This was all very nice, from his own point of view; but I heartily wished that he had to go first, to show me the right way of doing it.

"Oh, Jack, you are so brave," I said, "if you would only come with me, and make believe you had been sent for too, I should take it so very kind of you!"

"Don't you wish you may catch it?" he replied, turning round, to be ready for the path of retreat.

"Well, at any rate, come to the door," said I;

" to know that you are there, will be better than nothing."

"Oh bother, don't be such a funk,'" Jack answered; "why, Tommy, they won't eat you." And he took good care that they should not eat him, by bolting, as fast as his fat legs would go.

None of this tended to relieve my mind; but I tried to remember Achilles, and Hector, and all the brave men I had been reading of; yet in spite of them all, I took good care, so far as trembling hands allowed, to leave the door behind me open. It was now in my power, after fifteen years of growth, to go at such a pace with the wind behind me—and any wind blowing from a scientific point would surely find itself behind me—that if I could only get one yard's start, all the science yet invented—with the Devil at the tail of it—might break its wind without coming up with me. *Dat vires animus.* The whole of my *animus* was up and eager. I thought of all these wise men in our clot-pit; and out of despair I plucked hope, and defiance.

The longest dining-table in our hall, which would take thirty boys, and their plates, on each

side, had been proved to be not half long enough
for the length of the papers necessary for the
lantern jaws of science. Accordingly, three long
boards, upon which Dr. Rumbelow's Hermes
had cleaned our knives, had been brought from
his out-house, and set up, with green baize over
them, to carry ink and papers. Our new master
sat at the end of this length, with a brace of
Professors, on his right hand and his left. To
my innermost parts I recalled these four, and
was amazed to find that they knew not me.
Principal Crankhead waved his hand, for me
to stand silent at the bottom of the table;
and then they all turned round, and stared at
me, with the exception of Herr Chocolous, who
stood, with his chair pushed under the table,
to assert his upright principles. And he seemed
to me to be labouring not to laugh.

"The name of this pupil appears to be Thomas
Upmore," began Mr. Crankhead, "the son of
Bucephalus Upmore, a gentleman residing in a
place called Maiden Lane. Instead of expressing his preference for sixteen of the subjects
proposed for his study, he has stated very briefly,

that his father declines to pay for what he calls *extras*. He does not appear to have realized that these are the essential parts of all true education. Boy, what do you come here for?"

"If you please, sir, to be taught," I said, with a courage which surprised me, "to learn 'whatever is necessary for a liberal education,' according to what Dr. Rumbelow says to parents and guardians, in this paper." I pulled an old circular of the *Partheneion* from my pocket, and spread it on the table. "But father gave out, from the first, that he never would pay a shilling for extras; unless they agreed to take it out in soap."

"Take out science in soap, indeed!" muttered Professor Brachipod, forgetting how much he had done in that way; though certainly without intending it.

"Well, Upmore, tell us, if you can remember," Principal Crankhead went on, without deigning to notice old Rum's *prospectus*, "what are the *extras*, as you call them, which your father has refused to pay for?"

"Drilling, and drawing, and dancing, sir, and

washing, and French, and bacon for breakfast, sixpence a time for the delicate boys; and I think there was something about new-laid eggs."

" Zere is no sooch ting, I vill not allow it pass "—broke in Professor Chocolous, " vat you call ze new-laid egg have no right to be so called, because—— "

" Because it is generally stale, Professor. Well, Upmore, we seem to have ascertained what your father considered objectionable. But none of them belong to the domain of science. Your mind is a little confused, perhaps, as is only natural, at your age, after giving so much of it to Greek and Latin. Now take a fresh paper, and put your initials—we shall understand them —in the sixteen columns of your selection. Sit down, my lad; we shall teach you something yet."

Certainly my mind was now confused, neither by Latin nor Greek, but by the proximity of such a mass of learning, and its manner of foreclosing me. With a fog of big words spreading over my eyes, and pouring in at my ears, as I tried to sound them, I took up the pen

which had been thrown to me; then I put it
in my mouth, and said to myself—"it can't
matter much what I sign; I'll go in for the
biggest of the lot, to brag of them. Father likes
something that he can't pronounce."

There was no word of less than five syllables
there, and a good many of them went up to
eleven. These I picked out, to learn first, with
my thumb-nail, after counting upon all ten
fingers; and then I fell back on the deca-
syllabic branches of wisdom, and got my sixteen.
But, before putting anything down in ink—
which my father would have had to pay for,
unless he went down to the County Court—I
found in my mouth a little bit of the stuff (a
twisted, brittle, filmy stuff it is), which may be
the nerve of the quill for aught I know; and it
saved me most happily from knowing what its
name is.

For it got very easily into my throat,—so
widely was that poor throat agape, at the prospect of all those tremendous words—and I put
the feather-end in, to try to pull it out; and
then I began to chew the harl; and who ever did

that, without improving what he was going to write at first? Those gentlemen still were as eager as ever, that I should be shut up and done with; while I became unable to share their hurry, and desirous to see the case clearly.

"If you please, sir," I said, from the bottom of the table, after getting on a stool to be heard all up it; "the meaning of this paper is, that I am going to learn all this, for nothing."

Mr. Crankhead stared at the men of science, and with one accord they stared at him; and they would have been amused at my mistake, if it had not been too serious.

"Upmore, you have a great deal yet to learn;" the Principal spoke severely; "do you imagine that Science has ever imparted her blessings, for nothing?"

"I am sure, I did not know, sir," I replied; "but you said that all these were essential parts of true education; and old Rum says—Dr. Rumbelow, I mean,—in this paper, that all those are included in the money for the term."

"But we have changed all that, my boy. Our ideas of what education is are entirely different from those of the obsolete system, under which you have been trained hitherto."

"Then if you please, sir, my father ought to have had a new paper sent him, before he sent me back to school ; or how can he tell what he is to pay ?   I am sure, that he won't pay a farthing more than he had to pay last quarter."

"Thomas Upmore, you may go ; " the new Principal said, quite loftily, after whispering, and receiving whispers; " you need not return to the schoolroom at all, or to any part of these premises, except where your clothes and books are. You are too benighted, and con-tumacious, to deserve any higher education : such as you expect to get for nothing. Branker, see that this boy does not communicate with the other boys. Pack all his things up, and put him in a cab."

Thus was I discharged, very rudely as I thought, from the poor old *Partheneion*, now entitled the *Epistemonicon ;* and I could not help crying at the manner of it, because people would say that I had been expelled.

But Branker, the new man-of-all-work, who

seemed to care little about his place, at the sight of a shilling in my hand, allowed me to have a word or two, in the passage, with Jack Windsor.

" Jack, they have given me the sack," I said ; " because I wouldn't put my name down, for father to pay sixteen guineas extra. If I had, I should have been whacked at both ends, for certain. He would have whacked me 'for doing it ; and they would have whacked me worse, for not getting the tin. You have put down your dad for thirty-two guineas. Mind that, and I wish you luck of it."

" Stop the cab, Tommy ; stop the cab," cried Jack; "I'll come away with you, in five minutes. I must go in and tell them, I did it for a lark. Why, I should get double the hiding that you would. My governor has got such a host of kids."

I ran to fetch *Grip*, that he might run behind, and I waited in the cab, for about two minutes, and then out rushed Jack, without any hat on, and jumped in, and banged up the glass, and shouted, " Jarvey, off for Maiden Lane, as hard as you can go ! " Then we got out of sight in the back of the cab, and laughed, through the tears on our cheeks, at going home.

So it came to pass, that the boiling-interest was not represented any longer, in those halls of science. When my father heard what I had done, he shook my hand very heartily, and said that he never could have thought I had so much pluck; and he would not mind paying half again as much, but honestly, and on the square, you know, for my education to go on all right; and he would send them his bills, just to let them see what a sight of money their establishment had lost.

"And what language, I should like to know, was all that science to be put in? Elamites, Parthians, Medes, at least"—he said, as he looked at the paper of the fees—"to be any good value, for sixteen guineas."

"No, father," I answered; "it was all to be told us in English, every word of it; only very big words of course, such words as you couldn't make head or tail of."

"None the more honest for that," said father; "why, they make them out of their own heads!

I could do that, if I chose to try. Greek and
Latin is what I pay for; and this new lot don't
know nought of it. If it wasn't for my knowledge of the law, I'd have a defamation action
against them, for sending my only son home in
a cab like this, and not have the manners to
pay the fare! They have done the same thing
to Jack Windsor, you say. Every mouth in the
Lane will be full of it to-morrow. If John
Windsor would go snacks, I should feel half
inclined to consider about consulting a Solicitor.
And I believe it would pay; I do believe it would.
I am a public man now, and under Government
I act; and such a man should not have his
son kicked out, by a bunch of those dirty Professors."

"Bubbly, don't open old wounds," advised
mother; "our Tommy is come home, and I am
deeply thankful for it. How could they help
getting rid of him, when they never could have
taught him half he knows? They knew that he
had served his time with their master, the great
Professor Megalow; and how could they open
their mouths before him? And how could they

hold up their heads before Tommy, when they thought of the pit he led them into?"

"Aha, I see! That's it," cried father; "well, I musn't be angry with them after all. One good turn deserves another. And talking of that, we shall have no pits left, if what I was told to-day is true. The Vestry are going to send a man and two boys, all up through our valley, in the course of next month, with sticks and a line, to take measurements, and all the rest of it, for this drainage scheme. Well, it won't hurt us ; but I doubt very greatly whether the smell they are sure to make will be wholesome for my workmen. I must try to leave more of my stuff about, to keep the air fresh and the bad smells away. Sophy, I must be off; you might give me a nip of Hollands, before I light my pipe. And while I am at work, you and Tommy can put your heads together, concerning the next thing to be done with a young scamp, who has been expelled from school."

CHAPTER XVII.

SELF-DEFENCE.

It appeared to me now, that my education might fairly be entrusted to myself, at least until after Christmas-time; but whether it was, that my dear parents were eager to push me on with learning, or else that they had enjoyed enough of my company for the present, the issue was settled against me, and without another week of holidays. Jack Windsor was in the same box with me; and his mother and mine laid their heads together, and came to the conclusion that Dr. Rumbelow had acted very badly. With the aid of a noble "manual of epistolary correspondence," they indited a joint letter to the new bishop, which must have grieved his upright soul. He answered right humbly, and in few

words, that he grieved as deeply as they could
do, at the utter subversion of a wholesome school;
which would not have happened, if he could
have helped it.   But he had never been the
owner, and only acted under the will of Trustees,
who had not consulted him, when he left.   Feeling the deepest interest in his beloved pupils of
many happy years, he watched the result with
sad apprehension, but could not interfere with
it.   But for any, whose parents desired their
removal from the influence of wild doctrines,
he could with high confidence recommend an
orthodox, and most efficient teacher, an old pupil
of his own at Oxford, an accurate scholar, and
most active man, now doing excellent work in
the Church.   This was the Reverend St. Simon
Cope, curate of St. Athanasius, a District church
in Kentish Town.

Armed with this letter, the two ladies went to
see Mr. Cope; and came back in high feather,
perfectly full of him, and of new ideas.   I could
not understand their talk at all, and perhaps
that was more than they did themselves.   However, I made out that I was to get up at half-

past five next Monday, put a strap-load of Greek on my back, and knock, at half-past six exactly, at the corner-house in Torriano Square.

All this I accomplished, not without some groans, and was met at the door by Mr. Cope himself. I wanted to have a good look at him, but entirely failed to manage it; so wholly did my nature fall under the influence of his, that when I went home at night, and father said,

" Well, Tommy, what is the new chap like ? "

I could only answer, " I don't know. He is not like any man I ever saw before."

" Did he whack you, Tommy ? " went on my father: "you must want it, after all this time."

" He ! " I exclaimed with a lofty air; " he need never whack any fellow. I can tell that."

Of this wonderful man, it might truly be said, that he was wholly free from selfishness. Can anything, half so strange as that, be declared of any other human being ? That my own little body should go up into the air, is exceptional, though not unparalleled. But for the human mind to leave the ground, is an outrage on the laws of gravitation, ten thousandfold as rare as any I have yet accomplished. And now that I have time to consider it calmly, this must have been the reason, why I could not make him out, even with my outward eyes. And probably this was the reason, why we all admired, obeyed in an instant, and thoroughly revered him; and yet we found our spirits rise, when we got away to people more of our own cast.

This gentleman never was in a hurry, but always calm and gentle, and quite ready to be interrupted; yet the quantity of work he got through in a day was enough for ten men of his strength. Twice every day, he had service in his church, without even a clerk to help him, and four hours every day he spent in visiting poor people. Moreover, he always had in hand some article for the great Reviews, and a heap of other careful work; and besides all this, (and I dare say the hardest of the lot to deal with) a score of us day-pupils, to be taught, and fed, and tended. Yet never was one of us ready with a lesson, without the master being there to hear him. And he more than heard us; he poured his own mind, with all its clear and vivid power, as far into our thick brains as ever it would go, so that even Jack Windsor (who had no more taste in his head than a lignified turnip) told me, going home one night, that Horace was a fine chap after all, when you came to know what he was driving at. No other man in the world could have brought our Jack to that conclusion.

Now, in spite of all this, and the spending of every penny that he earned among the poor, the Reverend St. Simon Cope was not loved at all in Kentish Town; except by a few half-starving outcasts, and a good many ladies with nothing to do. And the reason of this was as plain as a pole—he was one of the " High-church parsons," whom the free-will of the Briton will never accept.

Under the care of this excellent man, I got on very fast in " Nescience," (as the *Episte-monicon* gentlemen called the classics), and history, and theology, and everything else except their own fads. From my very sad deficiency in weight, I never was a fighter, though often tempted grievously; but Jack Windsor was happily enabled to prove, that which has been proved perpetually in Town and Gown disputations, to wit, the clear superiority in conflict of the true Academic element.

For, as we came home about noon of a Saturday, with five days and a half of Greek inside us,—in a place where a bridge was, we were met, only Jack Windsor and myself, by a maniple—if they deserve the term—from the now adulterous *Partheneion*. These were fellows of the lewder sort, who had taken up gladly with all the new stuff, and were rank with all Chemical mixtures. Without looking twice at them, we could see they desired to give us a hiding. And they began the base unequal conflict, by casting very hard stones at us. With pleasure, and without disgrace (considering the force of numbers against us) we would have fled, by the road that had brought us ; but they had provided against this measure, by posting large boys behind us. There was nothing around us, but a world of thumps ; and the air was darkened with impending fists.

"Stop a bit; hold hard;" cried Jack Windsor, with his back against the coping of the bridge ;

" give us fair play, you lot of sneaking cowards.
I see a chap, who has been at our house, and
squibbed a wasp's nest with me. Let me speak
a moment to Bob Stubbs. Now, Bob, I know
you were an honourable chap, till you got among
dirty foreigners. I don't want to fight you, 'cos
we always were good friends. But pick out the
biggest of your scientific lot, and let me have a
fair turn with him; while Tommy here tackles
some fellow of his size. You must all be going
to the bad, up there; if you bring a score of
fellows to pitch into two. In the old days, we
always allowed fair play."

Being English boys, they were moved by this;
and after some little talk, two rings were formed
—one for Jack and his antagonist, and the other,
alas! for me and mine. Loth as I was to fight,
it seemed better than to be pounded passively;
and so I pulled off my coat, and squared up,
as my father had shown me he used to do. And,
whether by reason of his ancient system being
more practical than the new lights, or whether
in virtue of my own quickness, in hopping away
when knocked at, I may say, without any

exaggeration, that I hit the other fellow more than he hit me; until I was grieved to see him bleed, and then I put down my fists, and shook hands with him.

But my own little combat was no more in comparison with Jack Windsor's, than the skirmish between two charioteers of the " Iliad," while their heroes fight. Jack was in earnest, and knew no remorse. He had been hit on the forehead by a stone, and could swear that the fellow before him was the one who threw it. Moreover, this boy had shouted, " Come on, Suds!" with a most contemptuous toss of his head, being bigger than Jack, though not so strong, for our Jack was built up like a milestone.

"Come on, Suds," he shouted; "come on, my lad of lather!"

" I'll lather you, if I can," said Jack.

The battle was long, and quick with a spirit of trenchant valour, on either side. I did not see the beginning, because I was strenuously occupied with my own engagement; but that being brought to a happy conclusion, the boy

I had conquered joined me, with much good will, in observing the other fight. And here let me mention that his name was Bellows, Jeremiah Bellows of Blackpool, a prominent orator, as everybody knows, of the Liberal party, by and by.

When Bellows, and I, came up to look, there was no mistaking the nature of the fray. Very little time had been lost in repose between the rounds, and the action had been so vigorous, and so well sustained, that on either side now it was a harder job to fetch the breath, than to give the blow. Whichever might conquer, there could be no doubt, that the fight was a credit to his school.

Happily for us, the "noble science of self-defence" was not yet one of the thirty-two taught by the four Professors. Otherwise Jack would have long been vanquished, for he had not much of polemical skill; and I was astonished at his endurance, having always found him peaceful. But I knew, by the way his lips were set, and his square style of going forward, that his mind was made up, to be knocked to pieces, sooner than knock under.

This was a lesson to me, than which I have never had a better one in all my life. There was scarcely a pin to choose between those two, in the matter of affliction. Jack had got one eye quite bunged up, and his enemy had both eyes half-way closed; the nose of our Jack was gone in at the middle, and that of his adversary at the end; and their other contusions might pretty nearly match. Yet Jack won, all of a heap. And why? Because he would rather be killed, than yield. The other fellow would rather yield, than stand the very smallest chance of being killed.

So when Jack came up for another good round, his enemy sate, and looked at him, and thought it would be wiser to negotiate. He was not by any means whacked, he declared, and he went on to prove it, though still sitting down—as Britannia never lets her tail drop now, without elevating her tongue, to stand for it—but his mind was made up, not to incur further danger of blood-guiltiness.

After all the insults put upon him, Jack would not let him off, without a clearer understanding.

"Either you are whacked, or not," said he; "if you are whacked, say so straightforrard, and I will shake hands with you. If you are not, stand up again."

This was plain English, the only sensible thing in a case of that kind. The other boy looked about; but saw no way to shuffle out of it, having not yet been Prime Minister.

"I don't mean to fight any more," he said, "until I perceive the necessity of it. At the same time, you can see yourself, that I am not a bit afraid of you. Every one who knows me will bear me out in that. I could prove it, if I had time; but there goes the dinner-bell, and we all must run. Not from you, mind, not from you; only because we are obliged to bolt."

Likely enough, there are people who would be glad to make light of this victory; as they do with all those we always lose, while blowing up the trumpet in the very new moon, if ever we cannot help winning one. But Jack, and I, took a natural view of the facts we ourselves had created. Science had bitten the dust before the powers of ancient literature, though the latter had struggled at fearful odds; and seven of the boys, who had seen it, persuaded their parents to take them from the Gorgon, and apprentice them again to the gentle Muse, who only strikes in self-defence. And as soon as my father and mother heard it—by reason of my bruises, one of which required raw beef-steak,—they were for ever confirmed in their perception of their own wisdom.

But alas! I scarcely know how to tell the next event in my sad career. Gladly would I leave it all untold, save by mine enemies; if the latter would only tell it truly, or leave it untold falsely. But this it is hopeless to expect. There is a certain rancour in all persons of loose politics; wherewith—to put it liberally—nature, abhorring a vacuum, has stopped the vast gap of their principles. And this pervasive bitterness, when not obtaining vent enough, as it fairly might do upon one another, sometimes sets them raking up the private life, and domestic history, of those who are not like themselves.

It has been related, some way back, that the great authorities of our parish, having been urged by fussy people—most of whom paid no rates at all—to abate, what they were pleased to call, the nuisance of our wholesome smell, had arrived at last at a resolution, to cure the air of our chimney-tops, by carrying a big culvert through the valley, a hundred yards below. How this was to effect that purpose, none of us clearly understood; but as it would not come near our works, yet saved them from being grumbled at, we accepted the conviction of the public, that it must prove a perfect cure. And reasoning by analogy, we expected no stroke to be struck, for a score of happy years yet to come.

But Joe Cowl, that same chimney-sweep who had tried to summon father, told all his friends, till he quite believed, that he never had been the same man, since the time my father syringed him. If this had been true, how much it would have been to his benefit, and his neighbours'! But being scant of intro-spection, he positively made a grievance of it!

He contrived to push himself on the Committee appointed by the Vestry, for the drainage of Maiden valley, for no other reason in the world, than that he hoped to pester us, by carrying out that noisome scheme. As everybody said, there was no reason for such hurry; the valley had been a valley for more thousands of years than we could count, without wanting a bodkin put along it. In wet weather it drained itself; and in dry weather what was there to drain? The Lord had made it, as seemed Him best; and could any rate-payer improve His works?

Nevertheless, by stirring up, and rushing about with his best clothes on, and grouting (like a pig, with his ring come out) and writing, every other day, to every paper that would print his stuff, Chimney-sweep Cowl robbed all the parish of the pleasure of considering the next thing to be done. For he made them actually begin this job, at very little more than three years from the time of their voting it urgent, and not very much over two years from the time they raised the cash for it. But we let

him see, when it was begun, that we were rather
pleased than otherwise; and father went down
and told Cowl himself, with as pleasant a smile
as need be seen, that he would lend them a
spare wheel-barrow, if they would put new
gudgeons in; and as a large rate-payer of St.
Pancras, he would try to keep them to their
work. And it is a sad thing now to think of,
that if he had been a bad-tempered man, and
shunned them altogether, he might have been
alive, while I write this.

Perhaps no man in London, except the
Reverend St. Simon Cope, worked harder now
than my father did. Not from any narrow-
minded hankering after bullion; nor the common doom of our species, to find its final
cause, as well as case, in *specie;* but from the
stern resolution of a man, to turn out a good
article, at a good figure, and to keep his own
finger, and no others, in his pie. Mr. John
Windsor had been trying very hard, to dip his
own ladle into our warm vats; but while father
valued him most highly as a friend, and would
eagerly have done anything whatever, that lay

in his power, to help him : he found it lie more
and more beyond his power, to let him come
into his yard just now. Plump and portly as
Mr. Windsor was, and equally blunt at either
end, my father kept calling him—as soon as he
was gone—the thin end of the wedge, and telling
dear mother to be very careful, not to say a
word to let him in. This was exactly in ac-
cordance with my mother's own view of the
case; and she said, that she first had insisted
upon it, and that if Mrs. Windsor came sounding her for ever—as she did, even on a Sunday
—it would take her a long time to discover any
hollow place in her presence of mind. For she
always answered,

"Oh, my dear, what do I care for odious
business? You know, how much sooner you
would hear me talk, about delightful Happystowe, and the sun coming over the sea, and
the shrimps, and the shameful proceedings
of the bathing females—for I never can call
them ladies—and that dear good Lady Towers-
Twentifold, who longed so extremely to make
my acquaintance; and has written once more,

for my Tommy to go down, and spend the
holidays with his old friend, Sir Roland, at
Twentifold Towers. What a pity it is, that we
live so far asunder!"

"But don't you think, dear," Mrs. Windsor
asked demurely, "that when the wind was
blowing towards the windows of the Tower, her
ladyship might object a little to the—the
flavour of Mr. Upmore's operations?"

CHAPTER XVIII.

AH ME!

WHILE a fact is under fifty years of age, surely it is early days to despise it, as if in its dotage, and to traduce it as a mere tradition. Yet this was already, at the time I speak of, done by the wiseacres of Maiden Lane to the great, and well-established fact, that the Cholera. when it first appeared in the year 1832, had avoided—as if it ran away from the feeding smells, and pursued the opposite—every house, where a man could say that he ever tasted our chimney-stack. On the other hand, it had followed strictly, as on any good map can be shown, the main lines of the sewage system, so far as these could yet be traced. For as yet, they were very bold in places, and then vanished. without a mouth.

Now, if there had been any medical man, with power to think for himself—as certainly some do, in every century—he might have chanced to put these two facts together, and breed a conclusion. And the conclusion must have been—increase your chimneys, issuing a fine detergent smell, and abolish all drains, that bottle up and condense destructive odours, sending them out with a fizz at the traps, to rush into first-floor windows. But alas! there was no such man just then; and I fear that even now he is hard to find. Drain, drain, drain, was the cry of the period; and ventilate all your drains, that every one may smell them, and inhale a rich interest for his sewage-rate.

My father had never been blessed with any scientific education. He had thriven most stoutly, as his years increased, by dwelling in a feeding atmosphere. In an unwise moment, he convinced himself, that a change of inhalation would improve his lungs; which were as sound as a bell used to be, in the days when people knew how to cast them. The only fault anywhere near them was, that from the increase

of "adipose deposit," they had not the room to
swing, that in thinner years they had. But he
said to himself, and to my mother too—though
she had the sense to say 'nonsense'—that a
daily influx of entirely fresh odours would enable
him to holloa, as he used to do.

"Did you ever see Tommy look so well," he
asked, "as when he came back from the inside
of the whale? I require something of that
sort; and I shall go, and smoke my pipe, every
evening after tea, in the bracing air of Joe
Cowl's drain."

"That sounds very well," dear mother
answered, "but I do think, Bubbly, that you
ought to ask Dr. Flebotham first, what he
thinks about it."

To me it seems a sufficient proof, how grand
my dear father's constitution was, that for more
than two months he pursued this medical course,
as he loftily termed it, without any visible harm
to himself. And to the last moment of his life
—so stout and solid was his faith in his own
mind—he declared that his illness had nothing
whatever to do with the cause we assigned for it.

But after looking blue in the face one Sunday, and suffering from cold hands and feet, he came home at night, with a desperate headache, such as he had never felt before. My mother, in alarm, gave him brandy and salt; but he took the brandy, and left out the salt. On the follow-day, he was terribly sick, and as blue as the men at the Indigo works; and Dr. Flebotham pronounced it a case of aggravated English Cholera. He ordered strong measures to be taken at once, hot applications, and a bottleful of chalk, with opium in large quantities.

" We must not be nervous, my dear madam," he said to my mother, who was crying sadly; " our dear patient has an iron constitution, and great strength of will, and a rare fund of courage. Why, he won't admit even now, that there is much amiss with him; and nothing will make him stay in bed. The recumbent position is the one he should preserve, to give our therapeutic course fair play; yet he keeps on calling for his boots, and would go to his work without them, if you left the door unlocked. We must humour him, my dear madam; we must tell him that he shall go to-morrow to his most useful, and in many ways I am sure—delightful occupation ; without which this neighbourhood would lose one of its most—most pungent associations. Though Mr. Windsor certainly does, in his smaller way, make a much stronger st—stimulate our olfactory powers to even higher action, is what I mean. And it seems to be now very generally admitted, apart from all incontrovertible statistics, I may indeed say that it has been proved, *a priori*, by our new lights, that the chemical constituents, which you liberate by rapid evaporation, are for hygienic purposes the very ones which Nature has omitted to supply. But bless me, I have a lady doing well with twins ! You will remember all my directions. I shall have no time to dine to-day. I hope to look in again, at six o'clock."

He lifted his hat, and had scarcely time for me to run after him, and say, " If you please, sir, mother does so hope that you will not be offended, if we have a roast fowl on the table hot, when you come from the poor lady, with the two babies."

"Tommy," replied Dr. Flebotham; "that is the very first nourishment, your dear father should take, in a solid form. He must not touch it to-day, of course; but a very small slice, quite cold, to-morrow. It should be roasted this afternoon, and it must be excessively tender. It might be as well, for me to judge of that myself. It should be a large one, and yet very young— such as they call capons. Tell your dear mother, that I will try it for him."

"Oh, thank you, sir, thank you! How very kind you are!" I exclaimed, with the tears coming into my eyes. "Only please to be punctual at six o'clock."

He made this promise; and made it good.

"Unless the case becomes complicated," said the Doctor, three days afterwards, "with cardiac symptoms, or pulmonary, or possibly renal derangement, or any other resultant cachexy of the organisms; we may anticipate, my dear madam, a condition of gradual convalescence."

"Why, Doctor, he is ever so much better already!" my mother exclaimed impatiently; "he has ordered our Tommy to go himself, as far as the shop of the famous Mr. Chumps, and to try to be back by twelve o'clock, with three pounds cut thick of tender rumpsteak, and two dozen of oysters from Tester's. And he is coming downstairs, to dine at one o'clock. But he is so weak, that I shall have to help him. Deary me, what a thing to think of! And a week ago, he carried me up, when I slipped, and hurt my ancle. And I am not so light as I was, you know, sir. All that I leave now to my son Tommy. He will never be good weight."

"Very few medical men," replied the Doctor, with a pleasant smile at both of us, "would like to have the question of diet so completely taken out of their own hands. But as soon as therapeusis has re-instated our patients, though it be but a little, they are apt to think themselves quit of us. And then there comes the relapse, my dear madam; then there comes the sad relapse; and the blame of it is cast on us."

"He has taken a great many bottles, sir, such as I never could have believed;" my mother answered sorrowfully, "and it will be a little too hard upon him, not to let him have his change. How much will you please to allow him, sir?"

"Not an ounce, if I could help it—liquid nourishment for three days more. Our poor stomach is still most delicate, and unfitted for solid food. Restrict him, at any rate, to three ounces, and the like number of oysters."

This was easier said than done. My father got through a good pound of steak, and at least a dozen oysters; and after that, he felt so well, that he had a pint of ale, and some of his healthy red returned to him. My mother was so pleased with this, that she came to his chair, and kissed him; and he said,

"My dear. I thought at one time, I never should kiss you no more, nor Tommy neither. But the Lord has shown Himself most merciful. And I don't see, as a pipe would hurt me."

The next day, he was so much better, that at nine o'clock I went back to school, and worked with a light heart; trying to make up for the work I had fallen back with. And Mr. Cope

was most kind to me, and said that I did very
well.

I was let off, early in the afternoon, as mother
had asked that I might be; and with a good
wind at my back, I made my way home, at such
a pace, that every one turned to look at me; for
my lead had been laid aside, through father's
illness, which was weight enough. My mother
was equally short of breath, with pleasure and
excitement, when she ran out to kiss me. And
she said,

"Oh, Tommy, your father is as well as ever,
I do believe. He came downstairs without a
stick, and he wrote for an hour about something; and then he made a capital dinner,
and slept a little in the afternoon. And Dr.
Flebotham came and saw him, and said, 'My
dear sir, not too fast! You are getting well, at
a wonderful rate, but you must avoid excitement. You are not quite out of our hands yet.'
And then he turned to me, and said, 'We must
be careful of the heart, dear madam. The heart
has had a sharp trial, and has borne it well; so
far as we can see. But we must not be too hard

upon it, while its action is so weak. Any sudden
shock, for instance, might have very grave results.' Your father began to laugh at this, until
he remembered how very kind the doctor had been,
and so skilful. And then he begged his pardon,
and shook hands with him; and the doctor said,
'Not a bad grip that, Mr. Upmore, for a hand
that was like a swab, on Monday. Keep him
quiet, and he will do. Ah, I shall boast of this
case, a little; and I am sure you will help me,
madam.' And so I will, Tommy, though I never
can approve of being called 'Madam,' like a
Frenchwoman; for your dear father is in such
spirits, that he has taken an ounce of bird's-eye
with him, and gone to his favourite corner, by
the tree; where the wind brings down the smoke
so well, and what the people who write in the
papers call the 'pestilential fumes.' All he now
wants to set him up, is that, and a quart of
fresh-drawn stout; and he said, that he would
wait for that, till you came home from school to
fetch it. So don't stop now, to do anything, my
dear, except to put your slop-coat on, but run
down to the tree, and here is the eightpence—a

couple of Joeys, as you call them—and there's going to be a crab for supper. Tommy; such a beauty, from a friend of yours! I'll tell you all about it, when you come back, and you shall have his toes to suck, while you help me to do his cream."

I did love a crab, I always did. And as the greatest delight in oysters hovers over opening them (for no delight does more than hover), so of a crab, the finest hope is in getting him ready to be eaten, and in tasting stolen bits of him.

"You may look at him, Tommy," my dear mother said; and there he lay among lettuces, with his sweet legs clasped, as if in prayer for some one to come and eat them, and his fat claws crossed, in resignation to the mallet, or the rolling-pin.

It was not a sight to cause depression in the hungry human mind; neither could that effect be got from a very well-browned backstone cake; which mother allowed me to smell, before she put it back, to crisp a bit. Oh, if she had only said, "My dear boy, put your belt on," what a difference it would have made! But she never thought of it, any more than I did : and I always tried not to think of it.

With all these things to set me up, and a holiday and a half to come, out of the two ensuing days—for this was Friday afternoon— I set off, rather at a dance than walk, with my arms thrown up, and lungs expanded; and my broad-brimmed Leghorn giving flips at the wind, like a pigeon's wing; and the tucks, and gathers, and quilted flounces of my blouse lifting, and filling in the air, like clouds; and scarcely so much as a thread of my curls—as mother was fond of expressing it—that did not glisten in the sun, and hover like a crown of golden gossamer. Instead of opening the gate, I flew over it, and could scarcely keep between the walls below, and I heard mother calling,

"Oh, Tommy, dear Tommy, come back for your belt."

And I tried to do it; but the breeze was behind me, and I must go on. Then, where the old weeping plane-tree stands, at the bottom of

our garden and enjoys the smoke, there was
father on the bench, with his back against the
trunk, and his red plush waistcoat on, and a
long "churchwarden" in his mouth, and his
favourite pewter waiting for the stout, and his
face so bright at seeing me, that I called out,

"Father is quite well again! As well as he
ever was, in all his life!"

And he said—"Yes, Tommy, thank the Lord,
I am. I've been thinking of you all day, my
boy. Come, and give me a kiss. Why, how
wonderful you look!"

For the joy was more than I could bear; and
instead of being able to go to him, I was lifted
in a moment, from the surface of the earth,
quicker than I ever had gone up before. Now,
the faster I go up, the faster I go round,—this
seems to be a law of my ascents—yet I do not
remember to have felt much fear; and indeed
there was little to be afraid of, unless it was a
fall into our own chimney-stacks. And in my
vile stupidity, I even called down—

"Now, father, now will you believe at last?"

Alas, that my very last words to him should

have been of low, and unfilial triumph ! As I
tried to look down at him, through the tree, to
show him how comfortable I was up there, I
saw him rush out, with his pipe in one hand,
from the bower of the drooping branches; and
he stood, with his legs wide apart, and his hat
off, and threw down his pipe, and rubbed his
eyes with both hands, and then lifted them up,
and cried—

"'The Lord forgive me—that He hath made
a son of mine to fly ! '"

Before he had finished his exclamation, I could
see him no more, (because of the way in which
I was carried round,) and thus escaped the awful
shock of seeing my own dear father fall. And
before I could look again in that direction, the
briskness of the wind, which was north-west,
had taken me so far, that the plane-tree came
between, and I could not see the fearful thing
that I myself had done.

Yet somehow, or other, my mind misgave me,
that I had left some harm behind; and my
weight grew greater and greater; as I saw no
more of father, who ought to have run up the

hill to watch me, as people do to a balloon. This made me come down, at the bottom of our yard, when I might have gone over the Regent's Canal. My flights are always cut short by grief; but no other, by such a grief as this.

CHAPTER XIX.

COMFORT.

WHEN I came to know what I had done, through shameful levity, and heedlessness, and selfish triumph, and greedy ways—for that crab had much to do with it—also through laziness, and self-conceit, and the absence of humble gratitude —which would have taught me to fall on my knees, instead of skipping up like a bubble—for many hours I lay and groaned, and was much more likely to sink into the earth, than ever to mount into the air again.

My mother, in her first great shock and anguish, had called me a wicked boy, and said that I never ought to have been born; and I could only answer—

"Oh, how much I wish I had never been!

But it was more your doing than mine, mother."

I believe that I should have gone mad, after seeing the people come with father's coffin, if I had been left in the house, to hear, and think of all that they were doing. For mother was not at all strong-minded, but kept on falling from one condition of heart into the opposite; and sometimes cried by the hour, and sometimes laughed at herself, for the soreness of her eyes. And then it was so clear what father had been, by the way that every one spoke well of him— so gentle, and generous, and kind-hearted, and living entirely for the good of others — that instead of being comforted, I cried more, to think that it was I, who had destroyed all this. Several people took me by the hand, or patted my head, and made me look up at them, all of them seeming to say the same words, so far as I took heed of them—"Don't fret, my boy, don't knock under like that. It can't be helped now. Why, you did not mean to do it; and you must bear it, like a man, you know."

But all this only made me fret the more; my

heart was so broken that I touched no food, and
I kept on asking every man, who looked at all
like an authority, to please to get me sent to
prison for seven years' hard labour. Finding
no one ready to do this, I banished myself to
the coal-cellar, and had a fresh cry with the
maid, whenever she came to fill the scuttles.
For no one else came near me now, my poor
mother being unwell upstairs, and the command
of the house handed over to people, who called
themselves her nearest relatives; and were so,
if Uncle Bill had met with a watery grave, as
was supposed. These people were the Stareys
of Stoke Newington,—a widow lady, and her two
unmarried daughters, beginning now to be old
maids. Mrs. Starey was mother's half-sister,
nearly fifteen years the elder; and so her
daughters were my half first cousins, and might
have tried to help me. Mother said afterwards,
when she came to know of all their conduct,
that they did their best to send me after father;
and for a very good reason of their own—if I
were out of the way, they would be the nearest
to her (if Uncle Bill were drowned, as they had

reason to hope of him) and under my father's will that might be of no little service to them. But it is not in my nature, to believe that they would act so. And even by seeming so to do, they lost all chance of everything. So much wiser, as well as sweeter, is it in the long run for us, to be kind to one another.

But to dwell upon this, is hateful to me, and I cannot bear ill-will. Most likely the truth was simply this, that they had quite enough to do, with mother lying ill, and father dead, and could not be bothered with me as well, and therefore, were glad to be quit of me, saying that a boy's grief soon forgets itself. And if I did not eat, it was because I was not hungry; but time and youth would soon cure that. And perhaps they might have done so.

However, a man who was not in the habit of judging people harshly, the Reverend St. Simon Cope, was highly indignant with them. As soon as he heard of our sad loss, he thought he had a right to come and help us, as a minister of the Lord, though we were not in his District, and even belonged to another parish. Mr. Cope was

not at all the man to move his neighbour's land-
mark, and he knew that our parson (who never
came near us) was largely Evangelical, as the
people who went to hear him said. So that Mr.
Cope came to visit us, and was careful to put it
so, not as a minister of the Word, but as my
tutor in dead languages. In whatever capacity
he meant to come, no sooner did he see how we
were placed, than he threw parish boundaries
overboard, and became the true minister of
Christ. It is not for me to tell what he said;
·such matters are far above me. And in truth it
was less what he said than did, and his manner
of doing it, that moved us. I had thought him
a very cold man before—so little had he shown
of feeling, as perhaps was needful among boys,
but now brave tears were on his firm thin cheeks;
and I sobbed to look at them.

"Tommy," he said, as he drew me forth from
the coal which was all over me, and he never
had called me "Tommy" before, which made it
sound so kind to me; "Tommy, you must get
up, and wash, and take some food, and come
with me. Your dear mother is very poorly, and

I have promised to take you to her. It is the greatest comfort she can have; but she must not see you look like this."

"Have I been and killed mother too? Will mother die, sir, do you think, the same as my father did, through me?"

"No, my dear boy. Your mother will soon be well again, when she sees you. She keeps on calling 'Tommy, Tommy!' But they say that you refuse to go to her."

"They told me, sir, that she never would bear the sight of me again, as long as she lived. And she keeps on saying, 'Wicked Tommy, wicked Tommy, why ever were you born?' And I wish I never had been, sir."

"Listen to me for a moment, Tommy. Not one word of that is true. What she may have said at first, I cannot tell, and you must not think of; for she cannot have known what she said. I am sure, that you have a tender heart, and not a bitter one, my child. You have been afflicted heavily, and you blame yourself unjustly. Your only fault was sudden and thoughtless joy; and your mother sees that now.

She wants you to forgive her, for she behaved
unkindly, and she feels it. And if you wish to
make her well, go up, and see her, and give her
a kiss, and let her talk, while you say little.
Then she will get some sleep to-night; she has
not had a wink, since her sad shock. And to-
morrow, she will be well almost, and able to face
her sorrow calmly, for her illness is more of the
mind than body. But go, and do what I told
you first; and then I will take you to the door."

Thus it was that this good man saved us, or
me at least, from black despair, and consequent
insanity; for who can be sane, when hope is
dead? Everything came to pass, exactly as he
had foretold it; though I will not attempt to
describe what passed, between dear mother and
myself. Such matters are more for the heart,
than tongue. Enough, that when she was quite
worn out, with feeling things, and talking of
them, she fell into a smiling sleep, and I
smoothed the bows of her night-cap, and tried
not to believe how pale she was, and how many
little sheaves of silver grief had set up in her
fine dark hair.

Then, when she was fast asleep, after having managed, with my help, to get through a calf's sweetbread—which Mr. Cope himself went all the way to Mr. Chumps, to fetch for us—and there was no likelihood of her wanting me till morning, my tutor said,

"Tommy, you look respectable; which could hardly be said of you just now. Get your night-clothes, and whatever you want, and reverse the accustomed walk. Come with me to Kentish Town, and I will bring you back in a day or two. But I cannot give you much time to get ready, and you will have to walk six miles an hour."

If he had told me to take his hand, for an urgent appointment with the Devil, I should have done it, without two thoughts; but the only engagement he had to keep, was with his congregation. This was at eight o'clock in the evening; and counting me, and a baby, there were eight of us there for the good of it, without including the minister. This made me think, with a turn of tears, of a story my father used to tell, of his asking the Clerk at some church, why the Vicar had service at five o'clock of an afternoon on week-days, instead of seven, or eight, or nine. "Lord bless you, sir," the Clerk replied, "if we was to go into them long hours, we should never keep up with the time of day; five is our number at the outside, and no more." And although the joke was very small, it made me smile, as a bad joke does; when I never expected to have another smile. The service, moreover, did me good; though I never heard a word of it.

He put me with the other boys, next day; and they were very kind to me, knowing the trouble that I was in. Jack Windsor was not there now; because Mr. Cope had plainly told his father, that he found it useless to go on with him, unless there were any downright need of a standard to pass—and it must be a low one—for the Army, or for medicine, or for Holy Orders. For all lower purposes, his tutor said that he was quite up to the average: he could write and spell, quite well enough, and was up to the mark in arithmetic. But of Latin and Greek, if by great pressure, any more were ground into him, there was no chance of it staying longer, than the time his nails (which he was always biting) would take to grow, if he left off. Mr. Windsor answered loftily—for, together with his wife, he had always taken Jack to be a wonder—that he considered his son too good, by a d—d sight, for any of the lines of life Mr. Cope had been kind enough to mention, and he would take away poor Jack that day, and put him into his own office; where he would learn life, instead of burying dead languages.

Now, my dear father was in the habit of speaking his mind quite plainly; but he never would have spoken like that, so rudely; and sooner would he have bitten his tongue, very severely, I am sure, than have sworn, in the presence of a parson!

However, although Jack was gone, there were several fellows who had heard all, and a great deal more than all, about me, and my inborn affliction; and although they behaved with extraordinary kindness (being all on the way to be gentlemen) whenever they thought that I was not looking, they were looking at me, with desire

to form their own opinions silently, and compare them freely, when my back was turned.
For the result of any peculiarity, less conspicuous perhaps than mine, is to attract attention; and that becomes a curse far greater, than
the blessing of even the noblest gifts.

When the Doctor was kind enough to spare my
mother all the public pain of an inquest, by cer-
tifying "sudden death, from failure of the heart,
after violent attack of Cholera," it might have
been hoped, that outside strangers would have
gone on their way, without meddling. So all
right-minded persons did. They had their little
talk among themselves, and expressed a very
natural surprise, and agreed, or differed, according to the peace, or pugnacity of character.
And the matter would have been a nine days'
wonder, for the nine or ten beholders, but for the
prying self-conceit of a picker-up of news for the
Pratt Street Express, a penny paper, coming out
on Saturdays. I will not speak ill of this gentleman; for I came to know him afterwards, and
found him a pleasant, and well-meaning man.
He had no intention of inflicting pain; and he

freely admitted, that a sense of duty compelled him to write, what he did not believe a word of, lest a rival journal should get the start of his.

My tutor, Mr. Cope, sent a line to my mother on Tuesday, to inform her, that he thought it would be, for very many reasons, wiser that I should not be present, at the funeral of my beloved father. He did not tell me, that it was to be that day; and I did not venture to ask about it, leaving myself entirely in his hands. My mother wrote back, as it afterwards appeared, that she quite agreed with him, and would not expect me, until all was over. That same evening, he took me home, and asked me on the road, whether I could bear to hear a few words from him. I said yes, whatever he thought fit, for my heart was strengthened, while I held his hand.

After words of religious consolation, which fell from his lips, as if from heaven—for the whole of his life was above this world, and the preface to a better one—he proceeded partly as follows, though I cannot put it quite as he did—

"From all that I hear, and allowing much for large exaggerations, you have a remarkable gift, my boy; of which I heard something from my friend, the Bishop. From my own observation, I know that your bodily frame is of wonderful buoyancy; as your mind was also, until this sad distress, for the time, oppressed it. You have very good abilities, far above the average, an extremely tenacious memory, quick apprehension, with clearness of insight, and a love of whatever is elegant; which would make you a very good classical scholar, with industry, good teaching, and above all, good health. That last is the point, which makes me doubt the wisdom of pressing you much, in that way; although you have never known a day of illness, until this trouble fell upon you. For a body so light can scarcely contain the substance needful for hard work. But your duty, as to that, will depend very much upon what your father's orders were. He has left, (as I happened to observe) a statement in writing of his wishes concerning you. One of the ladies in the house had opened his desk, which had the key left in,

while looking for some paper, to boil the kettle.
And I fear, that she would have used this
important paper, in ignorance of what she was
doing at the moment, if I had not asked her to
put it back.   Then I locked the desk, and your
mother has the key.   It was not a will—your
mother has his will—but to you it should have
all the authority of a will.   These things are
important; but what I would speak of is, from
my point of view, more important still.   You
know, that whatever is given to us, is given for
some good purpose.   Your mental gifts are not
wonderful; although, as I have said, they are
above the average.   But your bodily gifts are
quite exceptional—I think I may say, though I
have never studied physics—and for them, you
will have a good account to render."

"But how, sir, how?" I asked with some
excitement; "as yet I have only come to trouble,
through all that.   Please to tell me any way of
doing any good with it."

"At present I cannot," Mr. Cope replied;
"but as sure as I am speaking to you,
Tommy Upmore, the way and the means will

appear, by and by. It is your duty, to improve your gift, so far as discretion and health permit, and to await the opportunity for some great good, to your country, humanity, or religion."

CHAPTER XX.

BOIL NO MORE.

THAT very evening, it was thought wise that the members of the Starcy family, who had come so kindly to our aid, should return to the bosom of their own affairs, at that pleasant place, Stoke Newington. My dear father was so widely known, and so loved and admired, by all the trade, that he received an exceedingly large funeral. My dear mother told me, how many high firms, nearly all of them wholesale, were represented; but I was pleased only because of her pleasure, or rather of the comfort she drew from it. Moreover, there were ancient friends who came, as well as still more of new date, and even some nephews of the name of Upmore, with warm recollections of their dear

Uncle, and hopes of a mutual (though post-humous) remembrance. Some of these had a good claim to be fed, in the hunger and thirst of unavailing sorrow—for none of them was down for sixpence—and my mother, who had made a great effort to attend, naturally left Mrs. Starey, and her daughters, to offer con-solation to these mourners. Among them, so deep a flow of sympathy was opened, that when Mr. Cope and myself came in, all the members of the Starey family, for our three had fetched the residue, were (as Mr. Cope said afterwards) totally unable *stare*. This made it incumbent upon us to send them home; and two cabs were ordered, with drivers of well-known integrity, who received the whole of them, and their goods, on condition of getting their money, as soon as their job was discharged conscientiously. Only they must get it from the people they took home, and not from those compelled to pack them off. Like all other sensible arrange-ments, this turned out to all reasonable satis-faction; though the Stareys made a fearful fuss about it, grieving to go away at all, and

still more to do it at their own expense. They
seemed to forget altogether, that when starvation
stared them in the face, my father set them up
in a small candleshop, and supplied them for
three months, on full credit. But such is the
way of the world; and what right have I to be
finding fault with it, while yet I continue to
belong to it?

When all this was over, and my mother gone
to sleep, I opened the paper which she had
given me; and with two of our own best candles
lit, (for my father would never have gas in the
house, to ruin our eyes and to disgrace our business) I read every word of it, sighing sometimes, and sometimes crying, to find how good
he had been to me, who had paid him out so
badly. And private as the matter was, the
public, having taken such a kindly interest in
me, might fairly call me ungrateful, if I shut
them out of all of it. Neither could that be done,
without a confusion arising between us. My
dear father had clear ideas, as to his own will
and way; and while he enjoyed himself much
in the world, he carried on his work to suit.

He had written a letter to me, to be read when he could no more talk to me; though he little thought, how soon that would be. After things which I need not enter into, he proceeded with these words, the whole being written in a plain round hand:

"You will see, my son, that I have worked hard, chiefly that you may do well. If anything happens to me of a sudden, as may be the case, after what I have gone through, your mother will be well provided for, as she has thoroughly deserved of me. Everything will be at her discretion; but I am sure that she will carry out whatever I wish concerning you. Cut no capers 'with my hard earnings; I think you have too much sense for that, and I have taken good care to prevent it. None of your high society nonsense, which is not fit for a tradesman's son; but a steady rise in the world, which is according to the laws of England. When the business has been well disposed of, after completion of all jobs in hand, according to the meaning of my will, you must go on with your school-learning, at the Oxford colleges, where

your friend Bill Chumps has done so well. I
have had a long talk with Mr. Cope, though
I did not tell your mother of it, and he says
that the money will not be thrown away ; for
it makes you anybody's equal, except among
the nobility. You have quite as good a head-
piece as Bill Chumps, if you will stick to it,
as he has done ; and you will see that it pays
as well to boil down animals, as to cut them
up, when a man understands the business.

" When you have been through the Colleges,
I intend to send you into Parliament, that you
may flabergast the Radicals. These are now
making so much bluster, and getting their own
wicked way so fast, that unless a firm stand
is made against them, no man's life will be his
own, no more than his land or money will.
Robbery is the beginning, and robbery is the
end of it ; and in the middle stands the man
with the biggest pair of jaws ; and laughs, as he
pockets all their thievery. If this goes on, a
man had better lie down on his back, and rant
all day, than labour hard, and be robbed of it.
You have heard me talk of this, my son ; but

we have only turned the first leaf yet; if Mr. Panclast gets the power he has set his stubborn heart on.

"Tommy, I am not a wise man, nor even to be called a clever one; but I am of a sort that is going by, and perhaps will be missed hereafter. That is to say, an Englishman, of common sense, and of fair play, and of tidy pride in his Country. All these are dragged in the dirt, by the people now getting upper hand of us; and what will come of it? They will drag themselves in the dirt, and their children; until our grandsons are ashamed to say—'I am an Englishman.'

"Now mind you this, my dear son, though you have little chance of doing it, fight you, tooth and nail, against the white-livered lot of Panclast. Who is he, by right of gab, and words no more English than himself, to upset the meaning of England, and the value of an Englishman? A change will come, among the changes he is always starting, when people will try to respect themselves; and finding it all too late for that, will turn against him, who has made it so. Then a very few men, without possessing any quality at all wonderful, except their love of their Country, may lay hold of the sense of our disgrace, and make it serve for common sense. Then good-bye to Mr. Panclast!

"Tommy, I wish that I might live, to see a son of mine bear share, in such an act of righteousness. But I hear your mother with the dinner ready, and I will go on about it, to-morrow."

*　　　*　　　*　　　*　　　*

The abruptness of this conclusion made me as sad almost as anything; although I do not see how my father, writing so much in pro-phetic vein, could have added anything of more precision, for my future guidance. I thoroughly understood his wishes, from the above brief sketch of them, and they agreed entirely with my own; so far at least as I had paid attention to such matters. Very few boys at school as yet, had made up their minds immutably,—as Sir Roland Twentifold had done already, and as every school-boy now does at once—what side in politics is the only right one, and how it may best be promoted.

As soon as we had the time, and spirit, to look round and think again, we could not help admiring, more and more, my father's wisdom. Not, by any manner of means, on account of the sum he had left for our benefit; though this turned out to be three times as much as my mother, in her most hopeful moments, had ever dreamed of finding it. It would be unnatural, if this had failed to increase her admiration; but she wished everybody to understand, that of that she thought nothing, in comparison with subjects so much higher. When coarse people said—" He has cut up grandly. My dear lady, I congratulate you, and your most interesting son, with all my heart;" she simply waved her hand, and said, " Sir, you can never have felt, as I do. Money is only an added trouble, when the guiding hand is gone, and gross exaggerations are made about it." And she felt most deeply the great injustice, and cruel hardship, of paying for probate a sum which made her weep again; because of the utter want of feeling, exhibited by the Revenue.

However, all this had one good effect, perhaps

contemplated by the Revenue. To some extent, it helped to turn the channels of her grief towards indignation, as well as compelled, her to look sharp, to baffle the harpies of the law, by all the resources of honesty. And so well did she manage, with the aid of Mrs. Windsor, (who became a very dear friend now, and entered into all her righteous feelings) that much disappointment, and many low suspicions, rankled in the stony heart of Somerset House.

But that, which my mother, and myself, and even the lawyer whom we were obliged to employ, found the most remarkable, was the skill and forethought displayed by father, in the settlement of all trade-affairs. I need not go into particulars now; any more than I need state exactly the value of his net estate. Upon that point, there are always people, who know ten times as much as the acting executor can discover, and are not to be put down, by any process of sworn arithmetic; though as yet it had not become the duty of any public journal, to measure the depth of a dead man's pocket, and tell the world, how he divided it. It will be enough, for those who care to follow my humble fortune, to know that Kentish Town, Camden Town, Islington, and Ball's Pond were wrong— though they all agreed about it, and, if any stranger doubted, doubled it—in putting it at considerably over the sum of a hundred thousand pounds.

With regard to the Works, my father had provided that any Government contracts, taken before his death, should be executed; and if any more were offered, upon like terms, his Executors should accept them, so long as the Conservatives remained in office. But if, as he clearly anticipated, the Kingdom were over-run shortly by Radicalism and robbery, the long-established firm of Upmore was not to be associated with them. For they cut down contracts to the uttermost farthing, and no honest man could work under them. In that case, our works must be offered for sale, upon certain conditions, and terms, etc., all of which proved his wisdom.

But nothing proved his wisdom, and clenched his words, with a sledge-hammer power, so much as the speedy result upon his proviso about contracts. For fear of spoiling my education, and attaching a soapy smell to me, it was strictly declared, that I must keep away from meddling with a business, which I did not understand. This alone will show the absurdity of the cries (now raised for party purposes) of "soap," and "dips," and "where's the grease-pot?"—with which I still have to contend, when I rise to address our enlightened operatives. My father had foreseen, I will not say all,—for no Jeremiah could have ever done that—but some of the mumbling, and blear-eyed decrepitude of the British nation, which now sets us longing to be Boers, or Zulus, or anything but what we unhappily are. And this foresight was shown in the result of the very next general election. The Radicals, (who are forced, by their own consciences, to set every other nation in the world before their own) came in with a rampant and blatant—the former to the friends of our country, and the latter to her foes—majority of six score at least.

No sooner was the result made known, with a mighty flourish of trumpets, and a proclamation of the Millennium, than a private and confidential circular was received by all substantial and enterprising Boilers. In it, the very ancient date of this typical firm was stated, as well as its rare advantages in position, and a thousand other things, including a vested right in Government contracts, and a certainty of being bought out, at a very noble figure, by the Committee of the new Cattle Market. Moreover, ashes were in great demand, for a newly formed Building-Company would take a million loads at once, to erect a thousand substantial villas, entirely upon, and for the most part of them.

Everything was going up and off, just then, like steam, and smoke, and bubbles mixed, as they used to be at our chimney-top. When a Liberal Government first comes in, it sets all knaves a-dancing; and even honest folk prick long ears up, at the infectious fanfarade of the great Rogue's March. There are certain to be, at once, bright summers, kindly winters, and vernal springs; and autumn will stand so thick with corn, that even the British farmer may have some hope, to get a gleaning. Trade shall

flourish, bubble-companies abound ; adulteration
—alone of British industries,—be subsidised ;
and every foreign bullet, fired into the back of an
Englishman, shall go back, ton for ton, in gold.

National securities went up, with the certainty
that they might be sacked, without outlay in
defending them ; and commercial circles squared
themselves, with the magic joy, which pre-
cedes the sure accomplishment of the impossible.
Every sort of investment was in demand, and
everybody expected ten per cent. on his capital,
without posting it.   Even Mr. Windsor, a stout
old Tory, fell into the rush of the Liberal flood,
and longed to buy my father's works ; but my
mother begged him not to do so, for she would
have been loth to see him disappointed ; and the
price was high. She told him of my father's
caution ; and he wisely saw its force.

I am heartily glad, that it was so ; for without that risk, our friend and neighbour lost as
much as he could afford ; when the usual relapse
set in, from braggart talk, and swindling promise.

But while these were new, and bright, they
served our turn, without fault of ours ; and a

Radical, of high faith, and sound cash, lost both —I am very sorry to say—in carrying on our fine old trade.

When these arrangements were complete, my dear mother carried out what she knew to be my father's wishes—though he had not found time to state them—by removing to a house upon Haverstock Hill, which stood in its own grounds, and saw as little of London as a " genteel villa " could wish to do; while the omnibuses passed our gate, every twenty minutes both to and fro.

Under the lawyer's advice, she bought this house, when she had tried it ; and then she set up a cook, and housemaid, and a boy to do the knives, and a pony, twelve hands high, to carry me, when he went quietly, or to pitch me off, when he was cross. And, whatever the weather was, every day, by 'bus, or pony, or afoot, I went to Mr. St. Simon Cope ; to learn the classics on week-days, and to hear him preach on Sundays. Until I became eighteen years old, and obliged to go to Oxford.

END OF VOL. I.

www.ingramcontent.com/pod-product-compliance
Lightning Source LLC
Chambersburg PA
CBHW030924050726
47498CB00003BA/884